A Whole New Light

Bantam Books by
Sandra Brown

Demon Rumm
Sunny Chandler's Return
The Rana Look
Thursday's Child
Riley in the Morning
In a Class by Itself
Send No Flowers
Tidings of Great Joy
Hawk O'Toole's Hostage
Breakfast in Bed
Heaven's Price
Adam's Fall
Fanta C
A Whole New Light
22 Indigo Place
Texas! Sage
Texas! Chase
Texas! Lucky
Temperatures Rising
Long Time Coming

A Whole New Light

Sandra Brown

DOUBLEDAY LARGE PRINT HOME LIBRARY EDITION

BANTAM BOOKS

This Large Print Edition, prepared especially for
Doubleday Large Print Home Library, contains
the complete, unabridged text of the original
Publisher's Edition.

A WHOLE NEW LIGHT
Loveswept edition published December 1989
Bantam paperback edition / August 1992
Bantam hardcover edition / December 2007

Published by
Bantam Dell
A Division of Random House, Inc.
New York, New York

Bantam Books is a registered trademark of Random House, Inc.,
and the colophon is a trademark of Random House, Inc.

ISBN 978-0-7394-9047-1

Printed in the United States of America
Published simultaneously in Canada

This Large Print Book carries the
Seal of Approval of N.A.V.H.

Dear Reader,

You have my wholehearted thanks for the interest and enthusiasm you've shown for my Loveswept romances over the past decade. I'm enormously pleased that the enjoyment I derived from writing them was contagious. Obviously you share my fondness for love stories that always end happily and leave us with a warm inner glow.

Nothing quite equals the excitement one experiences when falling in love. In each romance, I tried to capture that excitement. The settings and characters and plots changed, but that was the recurring theme.

Something in all of us delights in lovers and their uneven pursuit for mutual fulfillment and happiness. Indeed, the pursuit is half the fun! I became deeply involved with each pair of lovers and their unique story. As though paying a visit to old friends for whom I played matchmaker, I often reread their stories myself.

I hope you enjoy this encore edition of one of my personal favorites.

—Sandra Brown

A Whole New Light

One

Raisins, Cyn McCall realized, were actually nasty-looking things.

"Brandon, *please*."

"I like to do 'em this way, Mom, 'cause then you get to save 'em for last."

Cyn shook her head and sighed with resignation. Her mother heard the sigh as she entered the sunny kitchen. "What's going on? What are you frowning at, Cynthia?" Ladonia headed straight for the coffeepot and poured herself a cup.

"Your grandson is picking the raisins out of his bran flakes and lining them up around the rim of the cereal bowl."

"How creative!"

Cyn glared first at her mother, then at the puddle of milk that each misplaced raisin was dripping onto the table. "I was trying to correct him, Mother, not commend his creativity."

"Did you wake up on the wrong side of the bed? Again?" Her pause between the two questions wasn't accidental. It was Ladonia Patterson's subtle way of saying that her daughter's sour moods were recurring with unpleasant frequency.

Cyn pretended not to catch the gibe as she blotted up milk with a dishcloth. "Eat your toast, Brandon."

"Can I take it in the den and eat it while I watch *Sesame Street*?"

"Yes."

"No."

The divergent responses were spoken in unison. "Mother, you know I've told him—"

"I want to talk to you, Cynthia. Alone." Ladonia helped four-year-old Brandon from his chair and wrapped the slice of cinnamon toast in a napkin. "Don't drop crumbs." She patted the seat of his pajamas as she ushered him through the door, then turned to confront her daughter. However, Cyn got in the opening salvo.

"This constant interference when I'm trying to discipline Brandon has got to stop, Mother."

"That's not what this is about." Ladonia, slender, attractive, and fresh from her morning shower, squared off against her daughter across the breakfast table.

Cyn didn't welcome the imminent parental lecture, but she could smell one brewing as well as she could smell the coffee. She gave her wristwatch a cursory glance. "I've got to leave or I'll be late for work."

"Sit down."

"I don't want to start the day with an argument."

"Sit down," Ladonia repeated calmly. Cyn dropped into a chair. "More coffee?"

"No, thank you."

"You're not yourself, Cynthia," Ladonia began once she had sat down across from her daughter with a fresh mug of coffee. "You're uptight, edgy, out of sorts, impatient with Brandon. If I didn't know better, I'd think you were pregnant."

Cyn rolled her eyes. "Put your mind to rest on that score."

"What happened to your sense of humor? What's wrong with you lately?"

"Nothing."

"All right, I'll tell *you*."

"I thought you would."

"Don't get smart with me," Ladonia admonished, shaking her finger at Cyn.

"Mother, let's not repeat this conversation this morning. I already know what you're going to say."

"What am I going to say?"

"That I'm not living a well-rounded life. That Tim's been dead for two years, but I'm still alive, still young, with years of living to look forward to. That I have a wonderful job that I'm very good at, but that work isn't everything. That I need to cultivate outside interests and new friendships. That I need to get out, mingle with people my own age, join a single parents' club." She gave her mother a rueful smile. "See? I know it all by heart."

"Then why aren't you doing some of those things?"

"Because they're what *you* want. Not what I want."

Ladonia folded her arms on the table and leaned forward. "What do you want?"

"I don't know. I want . . ."

What? Cyn searched for an explanation for her blues. The element missing from her life wasn't so easy to peg. If she knew what it was, she would have filled the void a long time ago. For months now she had felt as though she were operating in a vacuum.

Brandon was no longer an infant who needed her constant nurturing. She felt ineffectual at work. Since moving in with them upon the death of Cyn's father, Ladonia had assumed most of the housekeeping chores. Cyn was the official head of the household, but the title didn't amount to much.

Nothing in her life produced a sense of accomplishment or satisfaction. Her youth and vitality were being drained by monotony.

"I want something to happen," she said at last. "Something that will shake things up, turn my life around."

"Be careful what you wish for," Ladonia softly advised her.

"What do you mean?"

"Tim's accidental death certainly shook things up."

Cyn was out of her chair like a shot. "That was a horrible thing to say." She snatched up her handbag, briefcase, and keys and yanked open the back door.

"Perhaps it was, Cyn. I didn't mean to sound insensitive. But if you want things to change for the better, you can't sit around relying on fate to shake things up for you. You've got to make a few changes yourself."

To that, Cyn offered no reply. "The traffic on North Central will be a nightmare, since I'm leaving so late. Tell Brandon I'll call him on my lunch break." Armored in righteous indignation, Cyn left for the hospital.

"I know that's what I said, George, but that was yesterday. Who could have guessed that they'd go public before—"

Worth Lansing signaled his assistant to pour him another cup of coffee. Her duties extended beyond clerical ones. Mrs. Hardiman was his secretary, assistant, mother, and pal—whatever the occasion called for. She was excellent in all capacities.

"I know that's my job, George, but you haven't lost—"

As his client ranted on, Worth held the telephone receiver against his chest. "Any other calls come in?" he asked Mrs. Hardiman, who was now watering the plants decorating his twelfth-floor executive office.

"Only from your dentist."

"What'd he want? I just saw him last week."

"Uh-huh. He looked over your X-rays and you need two fillings."

"Great, great." Worth expelled a long breath. "Got any more good news? You're sure Greta hasn't called?"

"Positive." She replaced the brass watering can in the cabinet beneath the wet bar.

"Well, when she does call, interrupt me," Worth told her, winking suggestively. "No matter what." She *tsk*ed him as she left the inner office.

Worth replaced the receiver against his ear. His client was still cursing the unpredictability of the stock market.

"George, calm down. It wasn't the right stock for you, that's all. Let me do some creative thinking here and get back to you before the market closes today. I've got a hatful of rabbits. I'm sure I can pull one out."

After he hung up, Worth left his red leather desk chair, consulted the TV monitor, which was constantly tuned to the stock-market channel, and picked up a scaled-down basketball. He shot it toward the goal mounted on the back of his office door. He missed.

No wonder; he was out of practice. It had been such a hellish week, he hadn't gone to the gym once, something he usually did religiously every day. This afternoon, he promised himself, before meeting Greta, he would treat his body to a hard, sweaty workout. He needed to be in prime condition for the coming weekend.

The information crawling across the lower third of the TV screen was getting more depressing by the second. He was still trying to decide what form that rabbit he had promised George was going to take, and desultorily throwing darts at the target across the room, when Mrs. Hardiman paged him on the intercom.

"Greta?" he asked hopefully.

"No, your lunch date just canceled."

"Damn. That old broad has got money coming out the kazoo," he muttered.

"I rescheduled for next Wednesday. Is that all right?"

"Sure, but I was counting on her fat portfolio to take up the slack this week."

"Do you want the sandwich shop downstairs to send up something for lunch?"

"Rare roast beef on whole wheat. Lots of German mustard."

Worth made a few calls, but was unable to unload George's stock onto another sucker. He called George, promising his unhappy client that he'd take care of it first thing Monday morning.

When the phone rang again, he lunged for it. "Yes?"

"They've already sold out of roast beef," Mrs. Hardiman informed him.

"To hell with it. I'll skip lunch." As he slammed the phone down, he asked the four black-lacquered walls, "Will this day never end?"

"Hi. Where've you been keeping yourself?"

Cyn's flagging spirits sank even lower as the doctor joined her in the elevator. She'd been dodging him the last couple of weeks. Most women, no matter their marital status, would consider her crazy for avoiding Dr. Josh Masters. He was good-looking, charming, and had one of the most lucrative ob/gyn practices in Dallas. He had delivered more babies in the last calendar year than any other obstetrician in the city.

More attractive than his other attributes was the fact that he was single and rich.

"Hi, Josh." She smiled up at him, but took a cautionary step backward. As close as he was standing to her, one would think the elevator was crowded, when actually they were the only two in it.

"Been avoiding me on purpose?" he asked, cutting straight to the heart of the matter.

"I've been awfully busy."

"Too busy to return my calls?"

"As I said," she repeated a shade testily, "I've been busy." She would never have wounded someone with a broken heart. Such wasn't the case with Dr. Masters. He suffered only from a bruised ego.

However, it had amazing recuperative properties. Undaunted, he asked, "How about dinner?"

Maneuvering around that, she switched subjects. "Listen, Josh, did you see that referral I sent you? Darlene Dawson?"

"I saw her yesterday."

"Thanks for taking her as a patient even though she can't pay. I would have sent her to the free clinic, but I'm afraid there might be complications with this pregnancy."

"According to her chart, she's already had two abortions."

"That's right." Cyn sadly shook her head over the plight of the unwed seventeen-year-old she had counseled. "She wants to have this baby and give it up for adoption."

"And you wanted her to have the best care." He leaned forward, trapping her in the corner of the elevator. "But delivering healthy babies isn't the only thing I do well, Cyn."

Dr. Josh Masters did not lack self-confidence. "Well, we're here." As the doors slid open, she edged past him and stepped out of the elevator.

"Wait a sec." He charged after her, caught her arm, and drew her aside, out of the flow of traffic on the ground floor of the women's hospital. Cyn's bailiwick was dealing with women who were seeking options to unwanted pregnancies.

She hadn't utilized her master's degree in psychology until after she was widowed. Marriage had come close on the heels of college, and Brandon soon after that. Within months of Tim's death, everyone had urged her to accept the job at the clinic, but, feeling unqualified, she had done so with reservations.

The hospital staff and the social workers who referred clients to her were enormously pleased with her work. She alone thought she was inept. Most of the cases she dealt with left her feeling depressed and ineffectual.

"You didn't answer my question," Josh reminded her now.

"What question?"

"How about dinner tonight?" He flashed her the smile that a cosmetic dentist had perfected for him.

"Tonight? Oh, I can't tonight, Josh. I left the house in a hurry this morning without spending any time with Brandon. I promised to do something with him this evening."

"Tomorrow night?"

"What is tomorrow? Friday? Well, I don't know, Josh. Let me think about it. I—"

"What gives with you?" He propped his hands on his hips and looked down at her with exasperation.

"What do you mean?"

"We had a couple of dates. Everything was going great, then you started stringing me along."

Cyn, taking umbrage, shook her shoulder-length hair away from her face. "I've done no such thing."

"Then go out with me again."

"I told you I'd think about it."

"You've had weeks to think about it."

"And I still haven't made up my mind," she shot back.

Encircling her arm with a caressing hand, Josh switched tactics. "Cyn, Cyn, look, we're grown-ups, aren't we? We're supposed to act like grown-ups. We're supposed to go out, enjoy each other's company—"

"Sleep together?"

His eyelids lowered lazily. "Sounds good to me." He used the seductive tone of voice that kept the nursing staff of the hospital, and many of his patients, aflutter.

Cyn withdrew her arm from his grasp. "Good night, Josh."

"That's it, isn't it?" he asked, falling into step with her. "The sex."

"What sex?"

"In our case, none. You're afraid of it."

"Hardly."

"You won't even talk about it."

"I talk about sex all day long."

Keeping his voice low, he stayed even with her as she exited the building and headed for the parking lot. "You can talk about it, but can't handle it when it comes around to you personally."

"I said good night."

"Come on, Cyn." He reached for her arm again, but she shrugged off his touch. "See? You get uptight if a man so much as lays a hand on you," he shouted after her as she hurried toward her car. "If the package isn't for sale, stop advertising it!"

By the time she left the parking lot, her hands had stopped shaking, but she was still seething. The doctor's ego was monstrous and insufferable. How dare he say those things to her just because she hadn't let their few dinner dates develop into sleepovers?

Stopping for the long traffic light at one of the city's infamously congested intersections, she propped her forehead on the backs of her hands while they moistly gripped the steering wheel.

Maybe Josh was right. Maybe she *was*

uptight about sex. Her healthy hormones hadn't been embalmed along with Tim, but she didn't relish sating them with just any man-on-the-make either. What did a nice, respectable widow with a child, in this age of safe sex, do with her sex drive when the object of her desire was no longer available?

Tough question. Too tough to sort out this afternoon. The day had started out badly at breakfast and gone downhill from there. What she desperately needed was to unburden herself to someone who would listen with an entirely objective ear.

To the annoyance of other motorists, when the light finally changed, she switched lanes and, instead of going straight, made a left turn.

"Good-bye and enjoy your long weekend," Mrs. Hardiman told Worth as he breezed through the outer office.

"I intend to. Take off early tomorrow. Don't hang around here until five o'clock. Get a head start on your Friday."

"Thank you. I will."

The elevator that silently conveyed Worth

to the basement parking garage was as high-tech as the rest of the building that housed his investment brokerage firm. He exchanged hellos and good-byes with the other young professionals who were leaving for the day.

Among them was a lady lawyer with legs like a gazelle and eyes like a fox. They'd been sizing up each other for months. He figured that next week would be an appropriate time to go in for the kill. He could coach a fox on how to be cunning.

Assured of eventual success with the long-legged lawyer, he whistled as he left the elevator and approached his sports car. His smile gradually faded when he noticed the envelope tucked under the windshield-wiper blade.

Before he even opened it and read the brief note inside, he had a foreboding that he wasn't going to like what it said. He was right. The concrete walls of the parking garage echoed his string of oaths.

"Great," he muttered as he slung himself behind the steering wheel and turned on the ignition. "That's just great."

It was almost sunset by the time he reached his high-rise apartment building on

Turtle Creek. As he'd promised himself, he'd stopped at the gym and worked out his frustrating day on the Nautilus machines and basketball court.

Pulling into the porte cochere, where a uniformed valet stepped forward to relieve him of his car and park it for him, he noticed the attractive woman standing at the curb, leaning against the hood of her car.

When she saw him, she smiled and waved. He waved back, retrieved his gym bag from the passenger seat of his car and tipped the valet, then jogged down the grassy incline toward the street where she had parked.

"Damn, you're a sight for sore eyes." He pulled her against him and gave her a mighty hug.

Cyn McCall rested her head on his shoulder and hugged him back. "So are you."

Two

Worth draped his arm across Cyn's shoulders. Together they walked toward the building's impressive and tastefully appointed entrance.

She smiled at the doorman as Worth ushered her past him and around the fountain in the atrium lobby. "I'd almost given up on you," she said.

"I'm glad you didn't. Been waiting long?"

"About an hour. Did you stop for drinks somewhere?"

"No, I went to the gym after I left the office."

In the elevator, they leaned against opposite walls and smiled at each other. She eyed his shorts and tank top critically. "The gym, huh? I was hoping you hadn't worn that outfit to the offices of Lansing and McCall. If so, I would feel compelled to criticize."

"If you came to bitch, you can leave now. You wouldn't believe the day I've had."

"Same here. I came to borrow a glass of wine."

"I think I can scare one up." Giving her a broad grin, he let her precede him out of the elevator and down the hallway toward his condo on the twentieth floor.

At the door, Cyn turned to face him. "Sure there isn't a girl waiting for you in here, up to her chin in bubble bath and prurient intent?"

"You think I'm that depraved?" He feigned affront as he unlocked the door and pushed her inside. "All you nubile, naked girls, clear out!" he shouted into the deserted rooms. "My conscience is here!"

"Heaven forbid. Being your conscience would be an endless, thankless job." She dropped her purse onto the entry table. "Almost as thankless as the job I've got."

"What's that I hear?" He cupped his ear. "A note of professional disillusionment?"

"Disillusionment, self-pity, and despair."

One tawny eyebrow rose crookedly. "I think this calls for *two* glasses of wine."

"Make them small. I've got to drive home."

"I'll get the wine and meet you on the terrace."

A few minutes later, he joined her there. She was leaning against the railing, gazing at the downtown skyline, several miles away, but seemingly close enough to reach out and touch.

The setting sun, to Cyn's right, reflected off the glass skyscrapers that distinguished Dallas and made it a tribute to late-twentieth-century architecture. The evening was cool, marking the beginning of fall. The sky was crystal clear, a passionate violet in the east and a raging vermilion in the west.

This spectacular view was just one reason Cyn had encouraged Worth to buy the condo several years earlier. Tim had told him it would be a no-risk investment. She had been thinking more aesthetically.

He handed her a glass of zinfandel. As

she took it, she said, "Whenever I come out on this terrace, I think of Tim."

"Why's that?" Worth sat down in a patio chair, removed his shoes and socks, and examined a blister on the ball of his foot, which he'd rubbed during his workout.

"I guess because he toasted you from this spot the day you moved in, remember? We opened a bottle of champagne—"

"*Warm* champagne."

"And drank to you and your health in your new home."

"You called it a pleasure palace, not a home," he reminded her, tipping his bottle of beer at her. "And after the champagne, you and Tim cleared out, leaving me with a condo full of packing crates and excelsior."

Smiling at the fond memory, Cyn reclined in a padded lounger. Setting her glass on the small table, she stretched her arms above her head. Before Worth had joined her, she'd shrugged off her suit jacket, tugged her blouse out of her skirt's waistband, and kicked off her shoes.

Feeling more relaxed than she had in days, she said with a wan smile, "You weren't supposed to remember that we deserted you."

"Are you kidding? I even remember your excuse."

"What was it?"

"You were still breast-feeding Brandon and it was time you got home."

"A valid excuse."

"Convenient," he quipped, "and unarguable. You mentioned leaking. That scared the hell out of me. I was afraid it could result in grave consequences."

"Like what?"

"How should I know? I'm just a dumb bachelor. Whenever I think of nipples, it's in an entirely different context."

Chuckling, she sipped her wine. "How's the brokerage business?"

"Lousy. The market's been in a slump the last three weeks. It'll be reflected on your statement, I'm afraid."

"I trust you."

The terms of Tim's will had left her with a percentage of the company's net income. She received reports on a monthly basis and deposited the dividends into a savings account for Brandon.

"I was supposed to have lunch today with a lady whose portfolio I've been courting," he told her.

"A lady, huh?"

"I'm talking old, Cyn."

"Like thirty-five?" she asked sweetly.

"No, like eighty-five. We had an appointment at a tearoom in Highland Park. You know, the kind of place where all the patrons have blue hair and white gloves."

"The men too?"

"Anyhow," Worth continued, frowning at her poor jokes, "she called and postponed."

"I'm sorry."

"Enough of my problems, how about yours?" He propped his elbows on his knees and leaned forward. "What's wrong?"

"I'm out of wine."

Mumbling his aggravation with her, he took her glass and disappeared into the living room. Lamps had automatically come on, courtesy of a timer. Through the wall of windows, Cyn could see him pouring her another glass of wine. It wasn't an economy brand out of a jug, but an expensive vintage.

Worth appreciated quality because he'd always had it, growing up the only child of affluent parents. Upon their deaths, he'd inherited a sizable nest egg. For him, Lansing

and McCall represented a challenge to suc-
ceed, not a means to make a living.

The condo was contemporary, superbly
furnished and immaculate. Worth had once
stopped seeing a woman because she left
the cellophane wrappers of the pepper-
mints she loved in the ashtrays. It was
laughable, Cyn thought, because Worth
didn't even smoke, and allowed no one else
to, so there was never anything else in the
ashtrays.

Worth was persnickety about his house,
his clothes, and especially his women. He
found something wrong with all the women
he dated. Too tall. Too short. Too thin. Too
plump. Too loud. Too quiet. Too ambitious.
Too lazy. Too pretty. Too plain. Too sweet.
Too hateful. Tim had given him hell about
how often he disposed of them, but in the
affectionate way that only a married best
friend can get away with.

"Okay, you've got your wine," he said,
handing it to Cyn when he returned to the
terrace, "and I've got a new beer, so what
gives? Why the long face?"

"I don't know, Worth."

"Come on."

"No, really. I *don't* know."

"Has my godson gotten out of hand?"

"Besides some strange eating habits, he—"

"Strange eating habits?"

"He arranges his raisins . . ." She raked her fingers through her hair, which the sunset had turned the color of melting caramel. "Never mind that. Brandon's not the problem. He's about the only thing I derive any joy from."

"Trouble with Ladonia? I can't imagine that. I would marry that woman in a minute if only she would have me."

"Worth Lansing, you are an unconscionable liar. You have absolutely no interest in any woman whose age or IQ exceeds her bust size."

"That's the second potshot you've taken at me tonight. Cut it out, or I'm gonna have to get nasty."

"Fire away. I can take it."

"Okay, remember you asked for it," he cautioned her. "If you aren't getting along with your mother, I'd lay odds it's your fault. That woman's a saint."

"I'll concede that our skirmishes are mostly my fault," she said tiredly. "It was my idea for her to move in with Brandon and me when Dad died, and I haven't regretted asking her to. Brandon gets to stay at home rather than being put in day care. Together we two widows have helped keep the loneliness at bay. I'd like to think I've bolstered her in the year and a half since Dad's been gone as much as she bolstered me when I lost Tim."

"No doubt you have."

"But she harps on me, Worth."

"Harps?"

"To get out and become involved in more than just work."

"You should."

"Don't start."

He set his bottle of beer on the table and took her hand. Pulling her into a sitting position, he wedged himself down behind her on the chaise lounge, straddling it with his long legs. Her bottom was tucked between his widely spread thighs.

"Hold this up." He scooped her hair into his fist and lifted it off her neck. "If anybody ever needed a neck rub, it's you."

"Hmm, thanks," she murmured when his strong fingers began kneading her tense muscles.

"Now, Cyn—"

"Uh-oh. Whenever you start a sentence with 'Now, Cyn,' it's always something I don't want to hear."

"I'm only telling you this because I know Tim would want me to."

"I knew there was a catch to getting a neck rub."

"Shut up and listen. This is your best friend talking. You obviously came here tonight for advice, and you're going to get some." He took a deep breath before plunging in.

"Ladonia's right. You need an outside interest. I know how much you loved Tim. I loved him too. He was the best friend and business partner any guy could ever hope for. He'll never be replaced."

He worked on her shoulders for a moment, easing out the kinks with his massage. "It never occurred to you that he'd get killed driving home from work one afternoon. You took it hard. Who could blame you?

"But, Cyn, sweetheart," he whispered, propping his chin on her shoulder and speaking directly into her ear, "that was two years ago. You're not even thirty yet. You've got to get on with your life."

"I realize that, Worth. There'll always be this little ache in my heart whenever I think about what was and will never be again, but I've come to terms with what happened to Tim. It's *my* life that I'm uncertain of and dissatisfied with."

"I thought you liked your work. Tim left you so well-off financially, you don't have to work at all. Didn't you once refer to the counseling you do as a labor of love?"

"It seems so futile."

"How can you say that? Troubled women come to you for help and you give it to them."

"Do I? I counseled one yesterday who's pregnant for the third time. The third time, and she's only seventeen!" she exclaimed. "She hasn't taken any of the advice I've given her previously. Birth control is free to her, but she won't take advantage of it. I might just as well be talking to a brick wall."

"You can't blame yourself for her actions. Your advice was sound, whether she chose to accept it or not."

"Intellectually I know that, but I get so discouraged. Another fifteen-year-old recently decided on adoption, but dreads going to school while she's pregnant because she's a cheerleader. She'd rather drop out of school than be unpopular. Another one cried for almost an hour today because she's afraid her father will kick her out of the house when he finds out she's pregnant, but she wants to keep her baby. Those are just the cases that come immediately to mind. I could go on all night.

"And what do I do for them? I sit there behind the security of my desk, dispensing Kleenex and platitudes, telling them I understand their problems, when I can't possibly understand them because I was fortunate enough not to have those problems. I feel so phony."

"You feel that way because you're not."

She glanced at him over her shoulder. "Is that supposed to make sense?"

"It makes perfect sense. If you didn't take their problems to heart, you would be like one of those wooden Gypsies in a glass box who sell fortunes for a quarter each. You'd tell them something that would make them feel better temporarily, then send them on their way."

"Truly?"

"Truly." He lightly kissed the back of her neck and started working his thumbs down the column of her spine. "Work may be the excuse you've given for this funk you're in, but I'd venture to say it's not the crux of the problem."

"Are we back to going out and mixing?"

"We are."

"Time to head for home."

"No way." He caught her by the shoulders and pulled her back against his chest. "How's your love life?"

"Hotter than a pistol."

"Glad to hear it."

She laughed, resting her head on his chest. It was broad, hairy, and only partially covered by his tank top. "Believe it or not, I do have an admirer."

"I can believe it. Who's the lucky guy?"

"I met him at the hospital. He's a gynecologist."

"No kidding? That's what I want to be when I grow up."

She gouged him in the belly with her elbow. "Pervert."

Around a grunt of pain, he said, "Tell me about him."

"He's handsome, charming, and rich. A real lady-killer."

"Hmm. I'm impressed. How long have you been seeing him?"

"We've been out a few times. Not lately, though."

"How come?"

"Because he's handsome, charming, and rich."

"Now who's not making sense?"

She asked, "What does a handsome, charming, and rich gynecologist want with me?"

"When he's already got scores of women panting to get in his stirrups."

"You're horrible!" She slid off the chaise and turned to confront him.

"I only said out loud what you were thinking." He did his best to look innocent, though a mischievous grin was tugging at the corner of his lips. His sparkling blue eyes belonged to a con man, urging, "Trust me."

"You're right," she acknowledged wryly. "That's exactly what I was thinking. He's only coming on to me because I'm one of the few he hasn't had."

"So, if you like him, let him have you." He assumed the relaxed position Cyn had earlier, resting against the back of the chaise, stretching muscled arms above his head.

"You mean . . . ?"

"Sure. It's simple. Just go for it."

"I can't, Worth." Having spoken with soft earnestness, she turned toward the skyline again, fully lit now against the darkness. "It seems so calculated and clinical to get into bed with a man who's practically a stranger just to have sex. The only man I've ever been with is Tim."

"I know."

She turned around and gave him an inquiring look.

"Remember," he said, "when the AIDS scare first started, you lectured me against having one-night stands. You told me I should find a nice girl and put a stop to all my sexual shenanigans.

"My argument was that there weren't any nice girls left. You said that you were a nice girl when you married Tim. I'm reasonably sure there hasn't been anyone since Tim, so I just assumed . . ." He gave an eloquent shrug.

She stared down at her stocking feet. "Josh says I'm uptight about sex."

"Josh?"

"The doctor. He said I could talk about sex with the girls I counsel, but that I wasn't secure in my own sexuality."

"His technique needs polish. Not a very tactful son of a bitch, is he?"

"I'm paraphrasing."

"Well, how about it? Is he right?"

There was a trace of defiance in her green eyes. "I'm as sexual as the next woman."

"Congratulations. Tell the doctor he's wrong. Better yet, prove him wrong."

"I can't, Worth," she said, her proud posture deflating several degrees. "So I guess there's an element of truth to what he said. I'd be uncomfortable on a date, knowing what was expected at the conclusion of it. My sexual mores are so outdated they creak, but I think more highly of myself than to be just another notch on an egomaniac's bedpost."

"How about starting a row of notches on your own bedpost?"

"Haven't you been listening, Worth? My problem doesn't stem exclusively from sexual deprivation. This depression isn't going to end the instant I go to bed with someone. It's more than that. It's . . ."

"What?"

"I don't know," she said with desperation. "Maybe it's the routine. When Tim died, I was advised to establish a new routine. Maybe I've stuck to it for too long. I need a change, a distraction, some spontaneity in my life. I told Mother this morning that I wish something out of the ordinary would happen, something that would—" She broke off when he bounded off the chaise. "Worth? Where are you going?"

"I just had a brainstorm," he called over his shoulder as he entered the house.

Curious, she followed him inside. Her bare feet sank into the sheepskin rug that formed an island of ivory plushness on the hardwood floor.

Worth unzipped his gym bag and took out his suit jacket, which he'd balled up and stuffed into it when he left the fitness center. He searched through the pockets until he found what he was looking for.

He returned to Cyn, slapping the crumpled envelope against his opposite palm. "The medicine that will cure all your ills is right here in this envelope, little lady."

He handed it to her. Giving him a look that clearly stated she thought he'd crossed the line between sanity and madness, she reached into the envelope and took out a slip of pink stationery.

" 'Darling Worth,' " she read aloud, " 'So sorry I can't make it. Unavoidable conflict just came up. Will explain next week. Love and kisses, Greta. P.S. Last weekend was fabulous. I shiver with ecstasy every time I think of—' "

He snatched the sheet of paper out of her hand and wadded it into a ball. "Not that."

"I was just getting to the good part."

"Will you please check out the other stuff?" he asked with asperity.

The envelope had a travel agency's letterhead. Inside were two round-trip tickets to Acapulco, Mexico. She looked up at him with misapprehension. "What about it?"

"Boy, are you dense. Check the date."

"It's today's date."

"That's right. Departure time, ten P.M." He squeezed her shoulders between his hands and, with a huge smile, announced, "And you and I are going to depart."

Three

"D-depart?" she stammered. "You mean me? Us? Together?"

"You. Us. Together. You and I, off on a weekend lark we both desperately need."

"Have you lost your mind?"

"Almost. That's why I need this weekend trip so badly."

"But what about Gretchen?"

"Greta. As her note said, something came up at the last minute and she couldn't go. I didn't know that until I was leaving the office. I was furious, thinking the weekend was a total washout." A wide grin broke across his face. "Then you came along and saved it."

Taking her hand, he dragged her across the room toward the telephone. "Call Ladonia and ask her to start packing your suitcase." He checked his wristwatch. "We'll have to stop at your house on our way to the airport. We've already got boarding passes, so we won't have to stand in a ticket line. We can go directly to the gate. I don't think we'll have trouble making it if we start now." He paused for breath. "Well, call."

Up till then he hadn't noticed that she was holding the telephone receiver he had foisted on her, but instead of dialing, was staring up at him, mouth agape. "Worth, are you nuts? I can't go to Acapulco this weekend."

"How come?"

"A million reasons."

"Name one."

"Work."

"They can do without you for one day. Ladonia can call in sick for you tomorrow and you'll be back on Monday."

"What'll I tell her?"

"Tell who? Ladonia?" He shrugged, his puzzlement plain. "Tell her you're going to Acapulco with me."

"I can't do that!"

"Why not?"

Clearly annoyed by his stupidity, she slammed the receiver back into place. "She's my *mother*. She'll think—"

"What?"

Cyn gnawed her inner cheek. "You might be accustomed to flying off to an exotic spot for a mini-vacation at a moment's notice, but I'm not. Nor is my mother used to me doing something so irresponsible."

"Look, Cyn, you'll be doing me a favor."

"A favor?" she asked skeptically.

"The tickets were a gift from Greta. She bought them as a special promotional package the travel agency put together. I can't cash them in. They're only good for tonight, with a return on Sunday night. I gotta use 'em or lose 'em, and that would be so wasteful. Would you want that on your conscience?"

She aimed an index finger at him. "When you smile that disarmingly, Worth Lansing, it's a dead giveaway that you're up to no good."

"If you don't believe me, see for yourself."

He handed the tickets back to her. She scanned the paragraph outlining the restrictions on travel; it confirmed what he'd told her.

"I'm sure you've got a list of sweet young things who'd dearly love for you to ask them on a weekend date to Acapulco."

"Sure," he replied candidly, "but not two hours beforehand, and not using another woman's tickets. Besides, Cyn—and you're going to find this hard to believe—I'm glad you're the one going, because with you I don't have to play a role."

"Role?"

"Prince Charming."

"More like Don Juan."

"Whatever. Around you, I can be myself. No games. No artifice. I can relax and be just plain me." To emphasize his point, he pressed her shoulders again. "That's what I need this weekend, total and complete relaxation."

"So why take along any extra baggage? Use one ticket for yourself and forfeit the other."

"The beach is no fun if you're by yourself," he whined. "Who'll catch the Frisbee? Who'll spread the suntan oil on my back?"

"I'm sure you could find someone to assist you," she said drolly.

"But I don't want to expend that much energy." He picked up the receiver again and, this time, punched out her phone number himself. "Come on, do something unwidowlike and impulsive."

Lifting the receiver to his ear, he drawled, "Ladonia, queen of my heart, how are you, love? . . . Yeah, I've missed you too, but I've been swamped with work lately. How're your mums? They weren't blooming the last time we talked. . . . Good, good. I'll be over soon to see them. Hold on, sweetheart, Cyn's here and she needs to talk to you."

Cyn was shaking her head vehemently and mouthing, "No," but he ignored her and extended the receiver, his palm cupped over the mouthpiece.

"Worth, this is crazy."

"Which is exactly why you should do it. Spontaneity, remember?"

Glaring into his smug face, she snatched the receiver from him. "Hi, Mother. Did you get the message I left on the answering machine? . . . Good, I didn't want you to wait dinner for me. . . . No, nothing's wrong. I just stopped by Worth's to say hello and, well, he got this insane notion that I should go to Acapulco with him for the weekend."

In preparation for her mother's volatile reaction, she clamped her teeth over her
lower lip and held her breath. But when she
heard what her mother had to say, her eyes
swung up to connect with Worth's. "You
do? Well, I don't. I think it's a ridiculous
idea."

"She's smarter than you are," Worth
commented, leaning forward and tapping
his temple with his index finger.

"What about work? . . . Yes, I suppose
you could call in sick for me."

As Cyn launched one objection after another, her mother shot them down like clay
pigeons. Worth signaled that he was going
into his bedroom to pack his bag. By the
time she hung up, he had returned, wearing
casual clothes suitable for traveling to a
tropical clime and carrying a small suitcase.

"She thought it was a terrific idea, right?"

Distressed, Cyn turned toward him.
"Worth, I still don't know about this. It just
doesn't feel right. What will people think?"

"What people?"

"Anyone who finds out."

He gave her his leanest, hungriest leer.
"You mean because you're a delectable

widow lady and I have such a notorious reputation where women are concerned?"

"Exactly. At least the part about your reputation. I shouldn't be leaving town with any
eligible bachelor."

"To you I'm not an 'eligible bachelor.' I'm
just Worth."

"But no one else knows that."

"Who cares?"

"I do."

He released a long sigh of impatience.
"Who's going to find out? If someone asks
you about it, just tell them you went to Acapulco with your best friend, which happens
to be the unvarnished truth. We don't think
of each other as sexual beings. You wouldn't
be hedging if I were another woman, would
you?"

"Of course not."

"Well, it's the same thing."

Looking at him from a purely objective
point of view, she muttered, "Not quite." Because, while he was her best friend, he was
most definitely a sexual being. He was also
extremely good-looking and as smooth as
frozen custard. She doubted anyone would
believe that traveling with Worth was a safe

and prudent thing for any widow under seventy-five years old to do.

"We've got to hustle. It's already after eight." During their conversation he had been securing the apartment. All that remained to do was set the alarm system as they went out the front door.

She caught his arm as he moved past her. "It's too late. Go on without me. I don't have time to pack."

"This is all I'm taking," he said, holding up his carry-on bag. "Half the fun will be shopping while we're there. Now, no more arguments. *Vámonos*." Giving her fanny a pat, he propelled her toward the front door.

After making a brief stop at Cyn's house to pick up the suitcase of essentials Ladonia had packed for her, they sped to the airport. Cyn had barely had time to swap her business suit for a pair of raw silk walking shorts and matching blouse.

Ladonia drove them so they wouldn't have the hassle of parking and taking a bus to their terminal. As they waited for their flight to be called, she promised to pick them up when they returned on Sunday night.

"Brandon, are you feeling all right?" Cyn pressed her hand against her son's forehead. "His cheeks are flushed. I think he's running a fever."

"He doesn't have a fever," Worth said, drawing her to her feet from her kneeling position in front of the boy. "If he feels hot, it's because he's excited over his new gun set. Hey, pardner?" He cuffed Brandon on the chin.

Brandon was wielding the toy six-shooter, twirling it on his finger, and sliding it in and out of the holster buckled around his hips. He beamed up at his indulgent godfather. "These're neat, Worth."

"And much too expensive," Cyn admonished. "You should have known better than to buy something in an airport gift shop."

"If Worth wants to buy Brandon a present, don't give him any grief about it," Ladonia said.

Worth pulled her into a fierce hug and noisily kissed her cheek. "I love this woman!" he declared. Ladonia basked in his affectionate attention.

"I suppose the new toy will keep Brandon

occupied while I'm gone." Cyn hadn't meant for her words to be overheard, but Ladonia had picked up on them.

"Don't worry about Brandon. I'll keep him so busy he won't even know you're gone. Don't think about anything except having a good time."

"I haven't been away from him overnight since Tim died." Cyn's expression was a blend of guilt and worry, universally maternal.

"The brief separation will be good for both of you."

"But what if he starts thinking I'm not coming back?"

Worth placed his arm around her. "Will you lighten up? Does he look concerned?"

Not only did Brandon appear unconcerned over his mother's impending departure, he was having a wonderful time firing his fake pistol at everybody from behind the cover of a waiting-area chair.

"You'd better get her onto the plane before she chickens out," Ladonia suggested to Worth when the attendant announced that the plane was ready for boarding.

"I was thinking the same thing."

Cyn tearfully kissed Brandon good-bye.

The only anxiety he expressed was over being hugged in public. He squirmed away from her long before Cyn was ready to release him. Her eyes were still moist when Worth took his designated seat beside her after storing their luggage in the overhead compartment.

"No tears allowed," he said sternly.

"I promise." She gave him a watery smile.

"Got your seat belt fastened?"

"All cozy, but I should have my head examined for letting you talk me into this. I'll be worrying about Brandon all weekend."

As the plane lifted off, he did a passable imitation of Groucho Marx, wagging an imaginary cigar and bobbing his eyebrows. "You've never been on a weekend getaway with me, doll."

"Don't you dare try to tease me out of this sad farewell scene. I promised not to cry, but I didn't say anything about melancholia."

He reached down and unexpectedly squeezed her bare knee. "Oh! Stop! Worth, that tickles."

"I know. You've always had ticklish knees."

"Cut it out. Ah!" She came up out of her

seat several inches when he squeezed her knee again. "I mean it now, stop." Batting his hands away, she began to laugh.

He placed both arms around her and nuzzled her neck, whispering, "You'll thank me for this on Monday. We're going to have a terrific time. Wait and see."

"Honeymooners?"

Worth raised his head, but kept his arms around Cyn. Both looked up at the inquiring flight attendant.

"Honeymooners?" she repeated. "We get a lot of them on this late flight."

"Uh, no," Worth said.

The attendant glanced down at Cyn's wedding band, which she hadn't yet weaned herself from wearing. "Ah," she said with a friendly smile, "you're old marrieds who're still in love."

"We, well . . ." Cyn foundered. "We're not married."

"She was my best friend's wife."

The attendant's lips formed a small round O. "Oh, I see."

As she moved away, they burst out laughing.

*   *   *

"They don't believe in wasting any light on the roads, do they?"

Cyn was plastered against Worth as the cabdriver took a hairpin curve at a speed that would make even non-Catholics want to clutch a rosary. From what she could tell of the landscape through the cloudy windows of the rattletrap, the road was bordered by a wall of rock on one side and thin air on the other.

"Be glad," Worth said as he repositioned his elbow against her chest, finding a place for it between her breasts. "If you could see out, you'd really be scared."

The car jounced; reflexively, Cyn grabbed his thigh and held on for dear life. "You've been here before?"

"Once. A long time ago. While we were at SMU."

"We? You mean Tim and you?"

"Yeah."

"He never told me he came to Mexico with you."

"That's right. He made me swear I'd never mention it to you."

"Why?" His grin made her eyes narrow suspiciously. "What did you do?"

"Boys will be boys."

The rattling taxi had picked them up along with six other passengers at the airport. They and their luggage had been crammed into the dusty interior of the vintage station wagon. Brass mariachi music was blaring from the radio. Requests that the driver turn down the volume had gone unheeded, because once fares had been negotiated and paid, he had conveniently forgotten his English.

"Do you feel like you're trapped in a deodorant commercial?" Worth asked Cyn.

The young woman sitting on the other side of him giggled. Worth had been on the receiving end of some sultry glances from her and her traveling companion, another young woman, since they'd spotted him on the airplane.

It hadn't escaped Cyn's attention that they made several trips each to the rest rooms at the back of the plane, making it necessary for them to pass their seats. En route, they'd ogled Worth each time. One had nearly mowed down the other in her haste to sit beside him when they were loaded into the taxi.

"It is crowded," Cyn told Worth in an undertone. "Sort of like a sardine can."

"But at least sardines are coated in oil before they're packed together like this."

"Now, that's an interesting thought." The comment came from the woman seated beside Worth. As she cooed the words, she pointedly looked down at his lap. Her friend gave a bawdy laugh.

Thankfully they got out at the first stop on the hotel circuit. "I think we're last," Worth apologized.

"It's not so bad now that they're gone. The knives of envy in my back were becoming uncomfortable."

"Huh?"

"Don't play dumb. You know they were lusting for your flesh and despising me on principle."

"It went a step beyond lusting," he chuckled. "Her boob was tucked into my armpit—and not by accident."

"Look, Worth, if you'd rather leave me at our hotel and pursue—"

"Don't be silly."

"I mean it. I want you to have a good time and not feel bound to me by obligation."

"They weren't my type, okay? Besides, I already told you, I'm not looking for romance this weekend."

"Sure?"

"Sure." He breathed a sigh of relief as the taxi wheeled into the hotel driveway. "This is us."

They were escorted into a pink lobby and served pink drinks to sip while they were registered by personnel wearing pink uniforms. Cyn removed the pink hibiscus blossom from the top of her glass and sipped through the straw.

"Hmm," Worth said, almost draining the tall, slender glass in one swallow. "I didn't realize I was so thirsty. How many of these do you think it would take to bring down a man my size?"

"Half." Cyn scooted her own drink aside. "One sip made my eyes cross. They certainly want you to have a good time while you're here."

"Señor Lansing?" An obsequious employee materialized beside them. "This way, *por favor.*"

The three of them crossed the naturally air-conditioned lobby, moving toward an outdoor driveway where a pink-and-white Jeep awaited. Their meager luggage had already been stowed in the back of it. Worth helped Cyn into the front seat, then climbed into the back. The driver engaged the gears, and like a thoroughbred coming out of the starting gate, the Jeep gave a lurch and charged up the steep hill.

In a blend of melodic Spanish and Pidgin English, the bellman/driver explained that the Jeeps served as the resort's elevators, transporting everything from guests to linens up and down the mountainside.

The winding road up the heavily vegetated mountain afforded ever-changing vistas of Acapulco Bay, the neighboring hillsides, and the city spread out below.

"I love it!" Cyn exclaimed. "The view is breathtaking. Oh, Worth, I'm so glad you talked me into this."

When they reached the summit, the driver parked the Jeep at a precarious slant. He retrieved their bags and nodded them in the direction of a white stucco dwelling surrounded by lush landscaping. The path was lit by flickering torches.

Smiling conspiratorially, the bellman escorted them through an iron gate and up to the door, which he unlocked and opened with a flourish and a graciously spoken, *"Bienvenidos."*

The suite was large and airy. It had a wet

bar and snack area in one corner, and a marble bath in the other. The sleeping area opened onto a private terrace with a spectacular view of the moonlit bay and the twinkling harbor lights. In the center of the terrace, a small, shallow swimming pool glittered like a magnificent jewel. Fresh hibiscus blossoms, as large as dinner plates, floated on the glassy surface.

While their bellman went around the room pointing out its many amenities and explaining the compartment that opened from two sides, where breakfast was left every morning without having to disturb the guests, Worth and Cyn stood like statues in the middle of the room, staring down at the bed—the one king-size bed.

Finally Worth looked across at her and gave a helpless little shrug. "As you said, they certainly want you to have a good time while you're here."

Four

Cyn tossed her purse onto the bed and propped her hands on her hips. This unexpected turn of events had overthrown her short-lived enchantment. "Now's a fine time to start joking, Worth."

"What else can I do?"

"You can ask for another room."

Worth turned to the bellman, who was hovering nearby, dividing his anxious gaze between the two gringos while wondering what had brought on their apparent consternation and imminent argument.

Worth slogged through his limited vocabulary of high-school Spanish. "Uh, *señor,* uh, *por favor* . . ."

"*Sí?*" The bellman stepped closer, eager to please.

"Have you got, uh, *tiene un,* uh, *una,* uh . . ."

"So far you're doing great."

"Well, you're free to jump in anytime," Worth said, rounding on Cyn when she dared to criticize.

"I took French."

"Great. If we ever get to France, that might come in handy, but right now I'm doing the best I can, okay?"

"Okay."

Worth turned back to the bellman, whose anxiety was increasing. "A room." He drew an invisible square in the air.

"*Las ventanas?*" The bellman pointed hopefully toward the shuttered windows.

"No, the windows are fine. We need another room. A room. You know, room? With two beds." Typical of a tourist unfamiliar with the native language, Worth's English adopted a Spanish accent, and he was speaking at a volume just shy of a shout. "*Dos,*" he said, holding up two fingers.

"*Dos?*"

"*Sí, dos* beds." He bent down and bounced the mattress a couple of times. "Beds. Two."

The bellman reacted with obvious incredulity. "*Quiere un cuarto con dos camas?*"

"I think so," Worth replied hesitantly. "*Sí.*"

The Mexican spread his arms wide and rattled off several sentences. Gesturing elaborately, he launched into a lengthy explanation.

"What did he say?" Cyn wanted to know.

"I think he said we're sunk."

"What?"

Worth raked a hand through his dark blond hair. "He said they didn't have any." Fishing into his pants pocket, he came up with a few bills of U.S. legal tender and pressed them into the man's hand. "Thanks, *señor* bellman. You've been a big help. *Muchas gracias.*" He shooed the baffled bellman out the door, then turned to face Cyn . . . and the music.

Her arms were folded across her midriff, her foot rapidly tapping the floor. Instantly Worth recognized her stance for what it was and raised his hands in the generally accepted sign of innocence. "I swear I didn't know."

"Why do I find that so hard to believe?"

"I swear, Cyn. It never occurred to me to check. Most hotels give you two double beds unless you request otherwise. How was I to know that this was honeymoon heaven? Greta might have known, probably did, but we didn't discuss the sleeping arrangements."

"With Greta, they didn't matter." Cyn surveyed the room with an appraising eye, seeing now what should have been glaringly obvious from the start. It was a lovers' paradise.

Sinking down onto the bed, which was sprinkled with fresh flower petals, she murmured, "The lobby was practically deserted except for those of us checking in."

"All couples."

"Did you see any families with children?"

"None."

"There wasn't a lot of activity going on."

"Not outside the suites, anyway."

She glanced up at him, then away. "Our gate had a 'Do Not Disturb' sign on it."

"And the bellman made a big deal over

the dumbwaiter where breakfast is left each morning."

"Hmm . . . the private terrace and swimming pool."

"The shower large enough for two . . ."

Their covert glances held for a second longer this time, and then they began to laugh. Worth laughed so hard he ended up sprawling on the bed beside her, holding his stomach.

"You should have seen your face when we walked in and you spotted this bed."

"You weren't looking any too poised, Mr. Lansing." She wiped tears of mirth from her eyes. "A rather inauspicious beginning to our weekend getaway."

"You can't say it's been boring, though."

"Certainly not boring." After she'd finally caught her breath, she said, "Before it gets any later, we'd better start calling the other hotels and locating me a room."

"Now, Cyn . . ." Worth sat up and clasped her hands between his.

"There it is again. The preamble that spells doom."

"Hear me out before you fly off the handle."

"If you're about to suggest that we stay

here together, save yourself the charm and the breath. I've got to get another room."

"Why?"

"Why?"

"We've shared a king-size bed before." Her mouth dropped open. "Don't you remember the weekend the three of us bunked together?"

After searching her memory, she clicked her teeth shut and shook her head stubbornly. "That was altogether different," she argued. "Tim was there and we were young and foolish and broke."

"We drove to Houston to see the Cougar-Mustang football game. After buying gas and food, we could only afford one motel room. It had just one bed and we all piled on. It was a helluva good time, but as chaste as church."

"I know, but—"

"It'll be that way this time too," he assured her.

"You're not thinking of inviting another couple in, I hope."

He shot her a retiring look. "We'll sleep in our clothes. I'll sleep outside the covers."

"No."

He groaned her name out of frustration.

"Why chase all over Acapulco in the wee hours looking for a room that'll be over-priced and God knows how far from here?

"And have you ever attempted to drive in the traffic down here? We'd spend most of our time trying to get together and not near enough time being together enjoying our-selves, which was the whole point of the trip.

"Besides, I wouldn't feel right about dropping you somewhere and leaving you alone. Resorts breed gigolos who stalk prey like you. I promised Ladonia I'd take care of you. She'd never forgive me if I deserted you."

His arguments were beginning to make sense, which worried her tremendously. "I don't know, Worth. If somebody—"

"Found out? What the hell do you care? You're a grown-up, aren't you?"

"Foul! Hitting below the belt."

"This is an adult situation. We're adults."

"Careful. You're beginning to sound like Josh."

"Heaven forbid." He pressed her hands, and pressed his point. "We can handle this intelligently, Cyn. For Pete's sake, I'm not going to chase my best friend's widow around a bedroom," he added in exasperation.

"I'm not afraid of that."

"Then what?"

"What if you want to chase somebody else around it?"

"Huh?"

"What if you meet a woman and want to bring her back here? Will I have to wait outside?"

"I could have brought a woman in if we were sharing a room with two beds."

"That's true," she conceded carefully.

"But that's not what I want to do. I've sworn off sex for this weekend. I just want to bunk with a buddy."

Through the terrace doors, she gave the private balcony a wistful glance. The pool was lovely, the moon gorgeous, the wind balmy, the view breathtaking. "It is a beautiful place. So much more than I expected."

"All right!" he said jovially, bounding off the bed. "You take that side, I'll take this one. Which drawers of the bureau do you want?"

He began unpacking his suitcase as though an agreement had been reached. Cyn supposed it had. It was dismal to think of spending the weekend in a city that was strange to her, in a hotel that couldn't be as wonderful as this one, among people who spoke another language, and trying to make connections with the only person who was going to make the trip any fun.

It had been silly to make such an issue of the one bed. As Worth had said, they were adults and could behave accordingly.

"You raid the snack bar while I'm changing." Taking a pair of swim trunks with him, he headed for the bathroom.

Cyn sat on the edge of the bed and thought wryly about her mother's warning to be careful about what she wished for. She had hoped for something to shake up her mundane, routine life. Well, once again she had gotten more than she bargained for.

"Delicious." Fifteen minutes later she was licking potato-chip salt off her fingertips. "How're the peanut-butter crackers?"

"Passable when you're starving. I wonder what time breakfast is delivered to that little box."

They were up to their necks in the silky water of their tile pool. They had demolished the entire stock of snack food in the pantry and drunk two bottles of soda.

"Hmm," Cyn sighed contentedly as she angled her head back and rested it on the rim of the pool. Kicking her legs just enough to keep them afloat, she gazed up at the sky. "Why aren't I sleepy?"

"Too much excitement."

"I guess. You'd think that—What was that?" she asked, sitting up.

"What?"

"That little squeaking sound. There it is again. I think it's those birds. Hear them?"

"Birds?"

Creating a tidal wave in the small pool, Worth climbed out. He went to the balcony railing and cocked his head to one side, listening and watching for the birds Cyn had mentioned.

She joined him there, shivering slightly inside the bath sheet she had quickly wrapped around her. The Pacific breeze was cool on her wet skin.

"There's one!" she cried softly, ducking her head slightly when one of the winged creatures swooped in low for an insect that buzzed around the security lights.

Beside her, Worth snickered. "Birds. Right."

"Well, what else?"

"We'd better get inside." He placed his arm around her shoulder.

She dug her bare heels in. "What are you laughing at?"

"Nothing."

"You're lying, Worth Lansing. What's so funny?"

"Your birds," he said, breaking into a full-fledged laugh, "are bats, love."

Cyn silently mouthed the word, then hightailed it toward the terrace door. Worth's hand shot out and grabbed a handful of retreating terry cloth, bringing her up short. He hugged her against him hard, laughing as she continued struggling to reach the safety of the suite.

"They're not vampire bats, Cyn."

"How do you know? What the hell do you know about bats?"

"Seriously," he said, his shoulders still shaking with mirth, "they're harmless, just out for supper. As soon as it starts getting light, they'll go home."

"Just like Dracula." She shuddered. He pulled her closer.

"They only attack human beings in horror movies. They'd rather have a nice fat juicy bug than your delicious blood."

She eased away from him. The towel slid to the terrace floor. "You're sure?" Fearfully she scanned the sky.

"Positive." Then his eyes opened wide; he bared his teeth and rolled his vowels like Bela Lugosi. "I, on the other hand, vant to bite your neck."

Which he did.

He attacked it teasingly, catching the soft pallet of skin beneath her ear between his teeth and holding on. Cyn uttered a squeal of fright and arched her back in an attempt to get out of his clutches. Both were laughing.

But their laughter abruptly ceased the instant his tongue touched her flesh. It had been an accident, but that didn't stop the contact from having an electrifying effect.

They froze, becoming immediately aware of their bodies. He had on a swimsuit, she a bikini, but it was the bare spots they were suddenly conscious of. Like her breasts swelling out of the top of her bra. And his corrugated, hair-smattered belly pressed against her smooth abdomen. And their legs perfectly aligned with each other.

The moment passed as fleetingly as their minds registered it. They awkwardly dropped their arms to their sides and separated. Cyn stooped down to retrieve her towel, nearly losing her balance because her senses were spinning so fast.

She fanned herself with a corner of the towel. "It's gotten hot."

"Very," Worth said in a voice that was little more than a croak.

"Coming?"

"Huh?"

"Inside?"

He swallowed hard. "Inside?"

She gestured toward the sliding glass door.

"Oh, inside, sure," he said around a loud, unnatural-sounding cough. "But you go ahead. It's your turn to use the bathroom first."

"I won't be long. I just need to, you know, brush my teeth and . . . and stuff."

Feeling foolish and not even knowing why, Cyn scuttled through the room and into the bathroom. The first thing she did after closing the door behind her was examine her neck in the mirror over the lavatory. Sure enough, there was a faint red mark just beneath her ear. Her stomach billowed and receded like a sail caught in a changing wind.

"You're acting dumb," she told herself crossly as she squeezed a glob of hair gel onto her toothbrush. Thankfully, she caught the mistake just in time.

As she punished her teeth with a harder-than-necessary brushing, she cursed Josh Masters for calling her attention to her sexuality, which, since she'd lost her husband, had been lying dormant quite nicely until about ninety seconds ago.

The whine of her hair dryer covered up the muttered lecture she gave herself for responding like an imbecile to a little kiss on the neck . . . a warm, wet, wonderful, world-shattering little kiss on the neck.

"It was Worth, for goodness' sake!" she said into the mirror.

Her reflection gazed back at her: same golden-brown shoulder-length hair that didn't take curl well, but looked best curving into a loose pageboy; same small triangular face, only now a trifle flushed; same wide green eyes.

But had it been Brandon's eyes she was gazing into at the moment, she would have checked to see if he were running a temperature. Her eyes had that glassy, glazed sheen that signaled internal fire.

Impatient with herself, she pulled on her nightshirt and left the bathroom before she could entertain any more foolish fantasies.

Worth's eyes went straight to her neck when she reentered the room, but the collar of her nightshirt covered the spot where he'd kissed her.

He had turned down the bed and was lying on it, stretched out on his back with his hands stacked beneath his head. His wet swimming trunks had been replaced with a pair of nylon jogging shorts.

"My turn?" he asked.

She nodded. He left the bed and went into the bathroom. Cyn got into bed and carefully arranged the sheet to cover her from her collarbone down, though the nightshirt was more than adequate. To occupy herself, she leafed through the entertainment brochures the housekeeping staff had left on the nightstand.

"Anything interesting?" Worth asked as

he emerged from the bathroom several minutes later.

Until he joined her on the bed, she hadn't realized how much she had missed the smell of damp, masculine skin. "Parasailing."

"I'm afraid of heights."

She set that brochure aside and picked up another. "A cruise around the bay with a stop for an island picnic lunch."

"Too touristy."

"A horseback trail through—"

"Forget it." Then, making a disgusted sound, he said, "Listen to me, shooting down ideas right and left. Do you want to do any or all of that? Because if you do, I'm game."

Before he even finished, Cyn was shaking her head no. "Doing nothing sounds best to me. No set schedules. I don't want to mark time. I want to lie in the sun. That's it."

"Good. Me too." He switched out the lamp. The bed rocked slightly as he lay down. He punched his pillow. "Maybe a cocktail cruise around the bay at sunset," he suggested once he had settled.

"That might be nice."

"We could check out one of the night-clubs."

"Sounds like fun too."

"Maybe get in some dancing."

"Dancing," she said dreamily. "I haven't been dancing in years."

"If you want to, we'll go."

"Whatever you want."

He was quiet for a moment before saying, "Cyn?"

"Hmm?"

"When did we start being so polite to each other?"

Uneasily she shifted positions. "Is that what we're doing?"

"Yes. We've been talking to each other like strangers ever since I kissed your neck." He rolled to his side toward her. "It was an accident, Cyn. A reflexive move-ment of my mouth. I swear."

"I know that, silly."

"Sometimes primal instincts take over. I mean, you're in a situation, like holding a woman in your arms, and these urges just come at you from out of the blue, and be-fore you know it, you're doing something you can't believe you're doing."

"I didn't give it a second thought, Worth."

"You didn't?"

"No," she lied.

"Oh. Well. Good."

He didn't sound convinced, or even pleased, but he rolled onto his back again. Cyn released a silent sigh that relieved some of the tension in her chest.

"Cyn?"

"Hmm?"

"Are you sleepy? If you are, just tell me to shut up."

"No. I'm fine."

"Well, I was just wondering if you miss . . ."

"What?"

"Sleeping with somebody?" He must have sensed her alarm because he rushed to add, "What I mean is, do you miss having somebody there with you when you go to bed every night, and knowing that he'll be there the next morning when you wake up? Do you miss knowing who that somebody is and what he likes for breakfast?"

This time she rolled to her side to face him. "Do I detect a note of regret for a life-style?"

"No. Hell no!" After a few seconds' pause he admitted sheepishly, "Well, maybe. I must be getting old. Or tired of playing the game. I don't know. I've just been thinking lately that the kind of relationship you and Tim had would be nice to share with someone."

"It is nice, Worth, to be secure in someone's love."

"Yeah, there's something to be said for monogamy, I guess. And having a kid together." He turned on his side, so that they were facing each other in the dark. "What's it like to have a baby?"

"Oh, it's a blast."

He smiled at her sarcastic reply. "I don't mean actually *having* it. God, how it must hurt. I can't even imagine," he said, shuddering. "What's it like to be carrying another life inside you?"

"You should know. Every time I saw you while I was pregnant, you followed me around begging to feel the baby kick."

"Well, I was an only child. I didn't have the pleasure of anticipating a little brother or sister."

She began laughing. "Remember the time we went to the movies and Brandon got rambunctious? I sat through the whole movie with him playing soccer against my ribs and your hand lying on my stomach."

"I didn't trust Tim to keep count."

"That's right! You had wagered on how many times the baby would kick before the movie was over."

"I won ten bucks."

"Fools," she said on a soft laugh. "Here I was with swollen ankles and a huge belly and the two of you were placing bets at my expense. The system stinks."

"True. In the reproductive process, I think men drew the better lot."

"You've definitely got the easy part."

"Funny," he remarked as he turned onto his back again, "I was sure we had the hard part."

Five

"You're sure it's okay?" Cyn asked anxiously as Worth assisted her out of the pink-and-white Jeep they'd rented at their hotel.

"Will you relax about the dress? It's dynamite."

"Widow ladies aren't interested in 'dynamite.' Leave dynamite to the nimble darlings on the beach, whose tummies haven't suffered the ravages of childbearing."

"Listen," he said, catching her by the shoulders, "I saw your tummy today, and I'd match it against any other on the beach. As for this dress, it looked great on the mannequin in the shop, and you can deny it till hell freezes over, but you had your heart set on it, and it looks fantastic on you, so stop fretting about it and enjoy it. End of sermon.

"Besides, if you were dressed like Whistler's Mother, it would damage my reputation as a ladies' man to take you dancing in this swanky nightclub."

"Are you always this cranky with your dates?"

"No. Only when they give me a hard time."

And only when his best friend's widow started making his mouth water.

"Have a little patience, Worth. I'm not accustomed to wearing backless dresses."

Worth placed his hand in the small of her back and guided her toward the neon entrance of one of Acapulco's famous discos. "It shows off the tan you got today."

"My skin is stinging a little. I think you missed a spot or two when you were rubbing on the sunscreen."

He didn't doubt it. He'd been behaving irresponsibly all day. It had started out innocently enough that morning. The joke he'd made last night had relieved the tension and put them back on track, so that they'd felt comfortable sharing the same bed.

They'd slept late and eaten a breakfast of Danish, fresh fruit, juice, and coffee on their terrace. Feeling perfectly at ease, Cyn had casually propped her feet up in one of the spare chairs. He'd had difficulty keeping his eyes off her long, smooth legs. And since when had a loose cotton nightshirt become the sexiest garment a woman could wear to bed? Maybe when it had caramel-colored hair lying tousled on the shoulders of it.

"Let me pay my part of the cover charge," she said now as a waiter led them through the crowd toward a table.

"My treat," he said tersely as he held her chair for her. He bumped his knee when he sat down. "I've eaten pizzas bigger than this table," he grumbled.

After the waiter had departed with their drink orders, Cyn leaned across the table and signaled Worth forward so she could make herself heard over the music.

"Are you in a bad mood? Don't feel like you have to entertain me. We can leave. I'd be content to just relax on the terrace tonight and watch the bats eat our bugs."

Their faces were close enough for him to count individual eyelashes. His eyes tracked downward from her beguiling smile to her throat, which had been given a glowing tint by the tropical sun, into the V of her neckline. He guiltily stole a glimpse of the slopes of her breasts.

"I'm in a terrific mood." Jaws clenched, he peeled his lips away from his teeth to form a travesty of a smile. He could tell she didn't buy it, but she was prevented from saying anything more when the waiter returned with their drinks.

Stirring the concoction of fruit punch and rum with the tall plastic straw, he mentally reviewed their day together. After breakfast, they'd piled their paraphernalia into the Jeep he'd rented and headed for the private beach made available to guests of the resort.

Without any affected coyness, Cyn had discarded her cover-up and charged for the surf. He'd followed her, reminding himself that this woman with the slender thighs and saucy bottom was a friend he'd known for years.

Worth had ribbed his roommate, Tim Mc-Call, about the Tri Delt he had the hots for. From the time Tim had worked up enough courage to introduce himself after their psychology class, Cyn had been all he talked about. Upon meeting her, Worth could see why, and had lauded his friend's good taste in women.

He had shown up with a six-pack and congratulations when Tim pinned her. He was best man at their wedding. While she suffered through labor, he'd paced the waiting room with Tim. Once he'd even watched his godson suckle at Cyn's breast. He and Tim had stood there gulping down unmacho emotions and trying to keep the telltale moisture out of their eyes.

But today, when she emerged from the waves, seawater trickling into her cleavage, and her nipples prominent beneath her bikini bra, he hadn't been touched by the spiritual beauty of her milk-giving breasts.

He'd been overwhelmed with carnal lust. It had slammed into him like a locomotive running full-out. It had propelled him through a tunnel of prurient fantasies as explicit as the porno flicks they used to sneak into the frat house.

He had a sick, sick mind.

It had misbehaved all day, not allowing him to ignore the fact that his late friend's widow was a beautiful, desirable woman. When she'd asked him to spread sunscreen on her back, his heart had pumped double-time, and all the blood seemed to flow toward his groin. Her skin was incredibly soft and sleek, the backs of her thighs supple, and he couldn't keep his eyes off her shapely derriere.

He was sick, all right.

Tim would come back and murder him if he knew the thoughts Worth had entertained about his wife today, especially as she twirled in front of him, innocently asking his opinion on the short white sundress. She had wanted it so badly but was intimidated by its blatant sexiness. He had approved and urged her to buy it because of all the skin it revealed and the way the soft fabric clung to her braless breasts.

Sick.

And now she was sitting across from him, her face drawn with uncertainty because he was acting like a jerk and she didn't know why. Her top knot was slipping, something she had complained about earlier. If she only knew how delectable those loose strands of hair had looked blowing across her face on the drive to the nightclub. If only she knew how damned enticing her fragrance was, and how appetizing her smile, and how alluring her— She would turn and run, and he couldn't blame her.

"Want to dance?" he asked abruptly.

"Do you?"

"I asked, didn't I?"

A rude jerk with a sick mind, that's what he was.

He reached across the tiny table and helped her from her chair. Taking her hand, he pulled her toward the dance floor, which was crowded with writhing, gyrating couples.

"I may be rusty," she said with an apologetic smile.

"Doesn't matter. Nobody's looking."

Nobody but him. And he was tuned in to every sensuous movement of her body. A subtle thrust of hip, a graceful shrug of shoulder, a gentle sway of breasts. He'd danced with her before, too many times to count, but always when Tim and he had switched partners. Until now he'd never really noticed what a good dancer she was. Far from being rusty, she was fluid.

The music beckoned everyone in the club onto the dance floor, until he and Cyn were jammed between other couples. His thigh brushed her pelvis; his arm glanced her breast. Compared to the sexual familiarity he experienced with most of the women he took out, those should have been inconsequential bodily contacts. Instead, they sent shafts of desire through him, causing pleasure, causing pain.

The Bon Jovi record ended and a Whitney Houston ballad began. Acting solely on impulse, Worth drew her into his arms. Just yesterday evening he'd massaged her back. He didn't even think of touching it now, but kept his hands decorously at waist level, until he saw another man on the dance floor give her a lecherous once-over; then he splayed one hand proprietorially in the center of her bare back.

Her hands were folded loosely behind his neck. He tried not to think about her breasts being pressed, soft and pale and full, between their bodies, but even that much thought brought a low moan to his lips.

She tilted her head back and looked up at him with concern. "You're not sick, are you?"

Very. "No. Why?"

"You're not acting like you're having a good time. Ladonia borrowed some pills from a neighbor that are supposed to combat Montezuma's revenge."

"My stomach's fine." Take it down about twelve inches, and there one would find the source of his problem. "I'm having a great time."

"Sure?"

"Sure I'm sure."

Smiling, he pulled her closer—just to ensure that he still could without reacting like a horny schoolboy. It proved to be a poor judgment call because their bodies fit together well—dangerously, deliciously well. Cyn noticed too. She drew herself up taut.

"What's the matter?" His voice sounded unnatural to his own ears. Probably because his face was no more than an inch from hers. He could see the spot he'd kissed last night. He could feel her breath.

He could feel her breasts. Her lips looked dewy and delectable.

"I . . . I guess I had too much sun," she said. "Or maybe the drink has gone to my head. I feel dizzy."

"Maybe we'd better sit down."

"Yes, maybe."

Even after agreeing on that, however, they made a few more revolutions on barely shuffling feet before he reluctantly set her away from him and guided her back to their table. Once he had her seated, he said, "Would you like some water?"

She fanned her flushed face with a cocktail napkin. "That might help. Bottled, please, but not carbonated."

"I'll be right back."

"The waiter . . ." She motioned vaguely.

"He takes too long. Stay put."

He plowed through the noisy crowd, moving in the general direction of the bar, glad for an excuse to be alone for several minutes. Maybe with some distance between them, he could sort this thing out. What the hell was happening here?

"One bottled water, please," he called out to a harried bartender.

"Hi, there."

Worth turned his head. Sidling up to the bar were the two young women he'd first seen on the plane. They were decked out for the evening in sequin tube tops. Their earrings were longer than their miniskirts. "Hi."

"Remember us?"

He rudely came back with, "Sure. Once a woman has poked her boob into my armpit, I never forget her."

They giggled, taking no offense whatsoever. "We saw you on the beach today."

"Oh, yeah?" He looked around for the bartender he'd given his order to. He was at the far end of the bar, mixing drinks.

"You must work out with weights," one of the young women said, socking him lightly in the gut. "You've got a great body. So . . . hard."

"Thanks. Hey, bartender, where's my water?"

"Where's your wife?"

"My what? Oh, she's not my wife."

One of the women gave the other a smug I-told-you-so look. "Really?"

"We're just, uh, friends."

"Where is she?"

"She's sitting down over there. She's not

feeling well." He flagged down another fleet-footed bartender by waving a five-dollar bill. "A bottled water, please."

"Guess where we're going later?"

"Where?" Worth inquired politely, distractedly, more interested in getting the water than in their plans for the evening.

"We're going on that tour that takes you to the nightclubs. You know, the *adult* ones."

His brows arched steeply. "Really? Well, have fun."

"Since your date's not feeling well, why don't you come along?" one boldly asked.

"I've already taken that tour."

"Is it as naughty as it's made out to be?" Lowering her voice, she asked, "Is it true that they really do it onstage?"

"You'll be thoroughly entertained." They were too caught up in the prospects to catch his derisive tone of voice.

"Oh, please come with us."

"Thanks, but as I've said, I've seen the floor shows already." He took the bottle of water and a glass from the bartender, who kept his five-dollar bill without offering any change.

"But it would be so much more fun with

the three of us," one wheedled, catching his arm as he moved away.

"No doubt it would," he replied wryly, "but count me out. Have fun."

Disappointment registered on both their faces as he disengaged his arm and plunged through the people standing four deep around the bar. Shaking his head with chagrin, he wended his way back toward the table where Cyn was waiting.

Except that when he reached it, Cyn was no longer there. It was occupied by another couple, who were exchanging smoldering gazes across two bottles of Mexican beer.

Worth made certain he had the right table, then asked the couple, "Excuse me, where's the lady who was sitting here?"

They glanced up at him, their expressions surly at having been disturbed. "Beat it," the man said.

"You must have seen her. She was here just a few minutes ago. White dress. Honey-brown hair."

"The table was empty when we got here," the woman told him.

"But—"

"Look, pal, if you misplaced your broad,

it's your tough luck," the man snarled. "Now, am I gonna have to call the manager?"

Worth set the bottle of water and the glass on the table and in the most explicit terms possible told the gentleman what to do with them. When a visual search of the dance floor failed to produce Cyn among the dancers, he plowed his way toward the entrance of the club.

Since he was swimming upstream, it seemed to take him forever to get through the crowd. He was winded by the time he made it to the exit.

Nevertheless, he sprinted toward the parking lot, where he'd left the Jeep parked. But as he streaked past the taxi stand, he pulled up short. "Cyn!"

She came around, obviously surprised to see him. "Hi."

" 'Hi'? Is that all you have to say?" His angry shouting drew attention to them from everyone queued up for a taxi. Encircling her upper arm, he pulled her out of line. "Why the hell did you split like that? Where are you going?"

"Back to the room."

"Without telling me?"

"You were busy."

"Busy getting you some water."

"I saw you talking to those girls again."

"I accidentally ran into them."

"Well, I thought—"

"That I was hitting on them?"

"Well, it wouldn't be the first time you've picked up women in a bar, would it?"

"Never two at a time!"

"Look, pal, if you and the wife are going to have it out, go someplace else. We don't want to hear it."

They had attracted a small audience. Worth snarled at the man who had dared reprimand him and, cursing beneath his breath, ushered Cyn toward their parked Jeep. "Dammit, don't ever scare me like that again," he said, giving her a hand up into the open car.

"For your information, Worth," she said huffily, "I'm a grown woman, perfectly capable of getting a taxi by myself."

"You are so innocent," he ranted as he twisted the key in the ignition. "Didn't you see the guys in that place undressing you with their eyes?"

"Undressing me with—"

"Yes! A good-looking woman alone is like

bait to sharks in a place like this. The way you move on a dance floor is as provocative as hell, Cyn. You probably didn't realize how many men you were attracting."

She stared at him, mouth agape, disturbingly reminded of Josh's parting shot about advertising what wasn't for sale. "I didn't do anything intentional to—"

"Which is why somebody's got to keep an eye on you. Don't run off like that again without letting me know where you're going," he lectured. "You had me scared spitless."

The traffic on Acapulco's main drag was slowed to a snail's pace. They got caught up in it. While they waited for a distant traffic light to change, young boys materialized from nowhere and began dusting off the Jeep and cleaning the windshield.

"I didn't mean to cause you any worry," she said. "I thought I'd be doing you a favor by simply disappearing."

"A favor? *Gracias, gracias,*" he mumbled to the boys, tossing each a coin. "Now, scram." He engaged the gears, but the Jeep rolled forward only several feet. A produce truck had broken down in the middle of the intersection, causing a gridlock in all four directions.

"I told you before we left Dallas that I didn't want to cramp your style," she said as Worth downshifted again. "You spent all day today entertaining me. First the beach, then with the shopping spree, then the cliff divers at sunset."

"I wanted to do those things too."

"I figured I would make myself scarce and let you enjoy the evening doing . . . well, whatever you had in mind to do with those two women."

He shot her a withering look and curtly refused to buy a blanket from a vendor who rushed forward, taking advantage of the traffic jam to peddle his goods. "I didn't know you had such a low opinion of me. I've done some wild things, Cyn, but the closest I've ever come to a *ménage à trois* was the night in Houston with you and Tim."

Damn! He wished he hadn't thought of Tim. Guilt was already eating at him for the thoughts he'd been nursing all day. When Cyn had disappeared, his first reaction hadn't been anxiety for her safety, but jealousy.

The thought of some other guy dancing

with her, touching her skin, enjoying her fragrance, had made him see red. What right did he have to feel jealous? Concerned, yes. Jealous, no.

The produce truck had been moved to one side and traffic was moving again. Cyn laid her hand on his thigh. He almost groaned out loud.

"My intentions were good, Worth," she said in soft apology. "I got the impression that you weren't having a very good time tonight because I'd been tagging along with you all day. I thought I'd conveniently disappear and give you a chance to . . . to—"

"Get laid?"

Her eyes connected with his briefly. She made a small assenting motion with her shoulders and quickly removed her hand from his thigh.

"Look, Cyn, if I want to get laid, I'll notify you first, okay? So until you hear from me to that effect, just assume I'm content."

"Fine."

Having left the city, they rode in silence along the shoreline road. It was the closest they'd ever come to having a serious quarrel. Neither was comfortable with the resulting silence, but Worth belligerently left it up to her to start another conversation. Eventually she did.

"What did they have in mind?"

"Who?"

"Those girls."

"A tour of the sordid nightclubs." He turned his head to gauge her reaction, and laughed at her expression, which was a blend of shock and curiosity. "Want to go?"

She blinked her wide round eyes several times, then leaned across the console and whispered excitedly. "Could we?"

Surprised, he hooted with laughter. "Are you kidding? And risk Ladonia's wrath?"

"She would never have to know."

"But if she ever found out, she'd skin me alive. I don't want to be held responsible for corrupting you."

"Do they really—"

"Yes."

"They *do*? Honestly?"

"Honestly. And that's all I'm going to say on the subject."

The last thing he wanted to think about was coupling. However, it seemed that was all he could think about while they played a game of gin rummy by candlelight on their terrace.

They laughed and teased each other, but he was miserable with guilt for wondering if she had put on a bra when she changed into the T-shirt she was wearing with a pair of shorts. Then when the cool breeze blowing in off the ocean proved to him that she hadn't, he was even more miserably guilty for noticing the distinct projection of her nipples.

After the lights went out, he lay stiffly on his side of the bed, keeping his back to her and cursing himself for being a lecher. Only a man with very little character could lust after his best friend, especially when she was totally unaware of it.

Thank God she was. Thank God she didn't know that he thought he'd die if he couldn't run his fingertips across her distended nipples, though he'd rather have his hand cut off than do it and offend her.

Thank God she didn't know that every time he looked at the faint rosy mark on her neck just beneath her ear, he had a vivid recollection of how her skin had tasted. As quick as the kiss had been, the flavor of her skin had left a distinct imprint on his brain. No matter how he had belittled the significance of that kiss last night, he wanted to experience it again.

His fantasies wouldn't be suppressed. Nor would his physical reaction to them. He finally became so uncomfortable, he left the bed, slipped through the terrace door, and stepped into the cooling waters of the pool on the terrace.

Six

The sound of splashing water awakened her. She left the bed and moved toward the sliding louvered door, which was standing open.

"Worth?"

He was crouched in the far end of the pool. "Did I wake you up? I'm sorry."

"What are you doing?" Realizing the stupidity of that question, she rephrased it. "Why are you swimming at this time of night?"

"I couldn't sleep."

"Is something wrong?" She moved to the rim of the pool, placing her bare toes right at the edge of it. He sank deeper into the water, until it reached his chin.

"Nothing's wrong. I'm just restless. Go on back to bed. I'll be in shortly."

She hesitated, halfway wishing he'd invite her to join him in the water. However, when it became evident that he preferred solitude to her company, she backed toward the door. "See you in the morning, then."

"Right. Sleep well."

When she stepped on something soft, she glanced down and saw that she was standing on the shorts Worth had been sleeping in. Realizing the implications of that, she swiftly returned to the suite, closing the door behind her.

The following morning, she couldn't stop thinking about his late-night skinny-dip. Her stubborn memory wasn't entirely at fault, however. Fate played a practical joke on her.

While they sipped their breakfast coffee on the terrace, they could see a couple in one of the suites on a lower level of the mountainside, cavorting naked in their pool.

Worth and she pretended not to notice, but both their gazes kept returning to the balcony beneath them. The pretense lasted so long, it became impossible for either of them to make a joking remark and dismiss the incident with a laugh. So they continued to stare.

The couple's affectionate playtime ended with a lengthy kiss. Eventually, wrapped up in towels and each other, they disappeared into their room.

Worth abruptly scraped his chair away from the table. "Take your time." Tossing down his napkin, he hastily left the terrace. Cyn joined him inside the suite a few minutes later. He had already donned beach attire and was gathering towels and suntan lotion.

On the drive to the beach, her eyes kept straying toward him. She became entranced by the movement of his muscular legs as he worked the clutch, brake, and accelerator of the Jeep. Had the hair on his legs always been that shade of gold, or had the sun bleached it out only yesterday while turning his skin a rich golden brown?

She commanded her attention to remain on the incredibly beautiful seascape, but for the duration of the ride her eyes and thoughts exercised a will of their own and stayed with Worth and his physical beauty and appeal.

He left the Jeep in the reserved parking lot. Together they trooped down to the beach. "What do you think of this spot?" he asked.

She checked the angle of the sun, the distance from the breaking waves, and the space between them and other sunbathing tourists, and nodded. "This is perfect."

He spread out their beach towels. She sat down on hers.

"Want me to put some lotion on your back?"

"No, thanks," she answered. "I'm going to work on my front today."

His eyes scanned her from neck to knee. In their wake, she felt a flurry of activity behind her belly button. "Did . . . uh, did you enjoy your swim last night?"

"Hmm. Sorry I bothered you."

She was bothered, all right, but not in the way he meant. When he stretched out on his back, his abdomen drastically curved downward from his rib cage. Cyn quickly averted her eyes from the stripe of body hair that tapered from his navel into the waist-band of his swim trunks.

"You didn't bother me. I never knew when you came back to bed."

That was a lie. She had lain awake long after he rejoined her in the bed. Knowing that he was lying awake too, she hadn't let so much as an eyelid move, but had lain rigid and tense.

"The swim relaxed me," he said. "I fell asleep almost instantly." The opaque sun-glasses covering his eyes also hid his lie.

She found it disturbing that not only had they started being inordinately polite to each other, but dishonest as well. When had their easy camaraderie regressed to the awkward pretentiousness of strangers?

She could pinpoint exactly when. Their relationship had changed when she had started noticing things like how his back muscles rippled whenever he pulled on or off a shirt, and the bewitching growth pat-tern of his chest hair, and the way his blue eyes sparkled when he smiled, and when she started experiencing pangs of jealousy every time she caught another woman look-ing at him.

That's why she had rushed out of the

nightclub the night before. True, she didn't want to be a hindrance to his enjoying himself, but she'd also had a compulsion to slap him and then go for the jugulars of the two flirtatious women.

Where had that come from, that she-cat jealousy?

No doubt Worth had intercepted her prolonged glances at him. He knew for a fact that she'd grown light-headed when he'd held her while they danced together. Hadn't his face looked tight and drawn when he led her back to their table?

Loyalty and chivalry kept him from dumping her, but that's probably what he had felt like doing. A widow who craved a man's attention was too pathetic to treat cruelly, so Worth had opted for kindly tolerance. She was making a fool of herself. He was disgusted by her behavior, but too soft-hearted to do anything about it.

She'd rather die than become an object of pity. Still, she seemed unable to help herself or reverse this embarrassing trend. And if the jealousy didn't kill her, the guilt would. She constantly fought the impulse to turn to Tim and say, "I'm sorry I suddenly can't take my eyes off Worth." The notion was foolish.

She was annoyed with herself for even having to acknowledge it.

Despite her best intentions, her eyes kept venturing to his prone figure beside her. Mutinously they wandered toward the notch of his thighs and the impressive bulge between them. Internal heat consumed her. Stifling a low moan, she hastily came to her feet.

Lifting his sunglasses, he squinted up at her inquiringly.

"I think I'll walk down to the market." She gestured toward the cropping of thatched-roof buildings about a half-mile down the beach. "I need to pick up some souvenirs for Brandon and Ladonia."

He started to get up, but she stopped him. "You don't have to go. You look so relaxed."

"Will you be all right?"

"Of course. You'll be in sight most of the way. I won't be gone long."

After pulling on her cover-up and grabbing her purse, she struck off on foot. She graciously declined to purchase marijuana, straw bags, ceramic bowls, and leather sandals from roaming vendors as she made her way down the shoreline.

When she reached the shopping area, the thatched roof provided welcome shade. The shops were junkier than the ones downtown where they had shopped the day before, but more fun because customers were expected to haggle. She easily killed an hour before leaving.

The sun was hot and the Pacific wind strong. She worked up quite a thirst. Before she reached Worth, she stopped at an open-air concession stand and ordered each of them a tall, icy drink, which would be delivered to them by a beach boy.

By the time she reached Worth, she was exhausted from walking so far in sand, barefoot, and carrying her handbag and purchases. Gratefully she sank to her knees beside him.

"Whew, I'm beat, but it was worth the trouble. I bought Mother a silver bracelet that she'll love. I couldn't resist buying one for myself too. I got Brandon a bullwhip. Think I'll regret that?"

Worth hadn't moved. He said nothing.

"Worth?"

His stomach was rising and falling steadily, indicating that he was asleep. Sitting back on her heels, Cyn observed him.

The wind ruffled his chest hair and lifted the dark blond strands that were lying on his forehead. Rivulets of sweat had run down his neck and collected in the V-shaped indentation at the base of his throat. There was the merest suggestion of a smile on his lips. A glance down his body readily revealed why.

"Worth?"

"Hmm?"

Snuffling, he took a deep breath, one that expanded his broad chest even broader. Still not fully awake, he raised his hand and laid it on her thigh, rubbing it up and down.

"Worth?" she repeated shakily. Her voice was so thin, the wind carried it away.

Gradually he came awake. "Hi," he drawled sleepily.

"Hi."

Then, realizing that his hand was gently squeezing her thigh, he sat bolt upright, snatching his hand away. "I, uh, must've been asleep . . . dreaming. Are you already back? What time is it?" Removing his sunglasses, he ran his hand down his face and, as casually as possible, flipped a corner of his towel over his lap. "How long were you gone?"

"A little more than an hour." Beyond his shoulder she saw the beach boy approaching with their drinks. She was glad to see him. Her mouth had been dry before, but nothing like it was now. "Thirsty?"

"Huh? Oh, yeah. Looks good. Thanks." He tipped the boy and took a long swallow of his drink. "I see you did some good," he remarked, nodding down at her package.

She repeated what she'd bought. He grinned at her mention of the bullwhip. "He'll be a regular terror with a whip and the guns I gave him before we left."

She groaned. "I didn't think of that."

"Guess I'll have to hike down there later and pick up a few souvenirs for him, Ladonia, and Mrs. Hardiman."

"I'll go with you. I know all the best places now."

"A haggler, are you?" he teased.

"The best. Or worst, depending on your point of view."

She dreaded pulling off her cover-up, but finally worked up enough courage. When she did, she felt exposed and vulnerable, demure and shy.

To cover her ridiculously unfounded modesty, she said with more enthusiasm than she felt, "Say, they've got horses you can rent by the hour. It might be fun to ride them on the beach. What do you think?"

"Sounds good. We'll check into it later."

But they never went horseback riding. They didn't shop for souvenirs either. The sun, the liquor in the drinks, and the peculiar mood that they shared, but couldn't account for, induced a delicious lassitude.

They whiled away the hot afternoon, lying close on beach towels spread side by side, and trying, without much success, to avoid staring at each other.

"Whatever you want to do is fine."

"You tell me."

"I don't care."

"You must have a preference."

They'd been going round and round on what to do that evening since they left the beach. Several options had been discussed, but so far a decision hadn't been reached. Each had showered off the sand and surf. They were currently sitting on their terrace, sipping cocktails Worth had mixed at their wet bar, watching the Pacific horizon swallow a giant crimson sun.

He was wearing shorts. Cyn was still in her post-shower robe. A towel formed a turban around her wet hair. Their bare feet were sharing a wrought-iron cocktail table.

"If you give them an hour's notice, the kitchen here will serve a candlelight dinner on the terrace. That way we wouldn't have to dress . . ."

Worth's suggestion dwindled when he caught Cyn's wide, apprehensive gaze.

"Or we could go out," he amended. "Here's a restaurant guide." He thumbed through the colorful booklet. "What do you feel like eating, ethnic cuisine or Continental? Seafood? What?"

"What about the restaurant here at the hotel?"

Worth consulted the printed material he'd carried out onto the terrace with him. "It's Continental, rates four stars, has a magnificent view of the bay, live music," he reported, reading from the brochure. "What do you think?"

"It would be a compromise. We could walk down and wouldn't have to fight the traffic again."

She didn't feel like a noisy, crowded restaurant and lots of people. But having an intimate candlelight dinner on the terrace would be sheer torture. She had wished for a ripple in her life, something that would rock the boring balance of it. But she hadn't counted on the catalyst being Worth. Nor had she bargained on a tidal wave instead of a ripple.

Thus far, she hadn't made a complete fool of herself, but being alone with him in this exotic and seductive setting might prompt an indiscretion she would long regret. Their friendship was too precious to risk.

Apparently he didn't want to be alone with her either. "Good idea." He slapped the pamphlet back onto the table.

"I'll have to wear the same dress I did last night."

"Fine." He shrugged indifferently as he left his chair. "Another drink?"

"No, but you have one while I'm getting dressed. It takes me longer."

"Why is that?" he asked in a free, friendly manner that was reminiscent of their relationship before they left Dallas. "Why is it that women take so damn long to get dressed?"

"Because men expect us to be gorgeous

at all times," she replied, matching his light-hearted tone. "That takes hours of preparation."

"Is that so? Well, you looked damn good when we came in from the beach a while ago, all windblown and sandy and sunburned."

Their eyes connected and held for several seconds too long to be comfortable. Grins gradually faded. "Thanks," she said awkwardly before ducking into the bathroom.

It was an hour later before they were dressed and ready. Against her deeper tan, the white dress looked even more spectacular than it had the night before. Worth wore a raw silk sport jacket over dark linen trousers and a pale pink shirt. Together they made a handsome couple. They boasted of it as they left the suite.

The restaurant was located at roughly the midway point of the resort, but it was still quite a distance to go on foot along the paved road that snaked up the mountainside. They hadn't gone very far when Cyn stopped.

"The heels must come off before I break my neck."

"Do you want me to go back for the Jeep?"

"No. It's a gorgeous night to walk, but I don't want to trip and fall. Good thing I didn't wear stockings." Using him as a prop, she removed her high-heeled sandals.

He smiled down at her bare feet. "Most women wouldn't be that practical. I like you, Cyn."

Laughing up at him, she asked, "Are you just deciding that after all these years?"

"Nope. I liked you the first time Tim introduced us." Leaning down, he added teasingly, "And I didn't even know then that you floss every night."

"Two can play this game, Mr. Lansing." Her eyes narrowed into green slits. "Do you always start out with a pillow and end up throwing it to the foot of the bed by morning?"

"How long have you had that bunion on the ball of your left foot?"

"When did you start using baby shampoo?"

"Now, now. If you start disparaging my baby shampoo, I'll have to get mean."

"Like what?" she taunted.

"Like citing that you use lemon juice to

keep these strands of hair around your face lighter than the rest," he said, tugging on one that had slipped from her ponytail.

"So you think you know all my beauty secrets now?" Laughing, they came together in a hug. "I like you, too, Worth."

When they separated, he took her hand, and, swinging their arms companionably between them, they continued their walk to the restaurant. At the entrance, Cyn slipped on her shoes before being shown to an outdoor table that overlooked the bay and the city, which spread around the harbor like a jeweled fan.

The flame inside the lantern on their table danced with every breath of ocean air. Lightning flickered periodically behind neighboring mountains, but their deferential waiter assured them that it wouldn't rain for hours. The thunder was friendly, not ominous. Lilting music from a harpist and flutist provided a soothing background for deliciously prepared Continental food and easy conversation.

It faltered only whenever their eyes happened to meet.

"You may have to roll me up this hill," Cyn groaned as they left the restaurant. "The food was too good to leave a single morsel."

He supported her while she removed her shoes again. Taking them from her, he slipped one into each of the pockets of his jacket.

"There's no rush to get back," he said as they began walking again. "We can take our time."

That's what they did. They dawdled along the way, stopping periodically to enjoy the varying views provided by the twisting road.

One vista was particularly worth savoring, since it encompassed the entire bay and the city. They sat on a low stone wall to enjoy the panorama. The wind caressed them, molding Cyn's dress to her body. To feel the fabric fluttering against her skin was a sensual delight, but she self-consciously folded her arms over her breasts.

"It's so beautiful." She sighed. "Thank you for insisting that I come, Worth."

"The pleasure's been all mine." His voice sounded thick. She whipped her head around and caught him looking at the breasts she was trying to conceal.

"I've loved every minute of it."

"Have you, Cyn?"

"Yes."

"Good. That's why we came."

"The problems waiting for me back in Dallas seem far away. From way up here, I feel separated from reality."

He formed a pained expression. "Please don't point out how high up we are. Remember my fear of heights."

She pushed strands of windblown hair out of her eyes. Her ponytail was no longer intact. "If you're afraid of heights, why do you live in a high-rise?"

"I never stand next to the terrace railing like you were doing the other night. As long as I can look out and not straight down, I'm okay. It's the feeling of suspension that gets me."

"You didn't seem to have any trouble on the flight down here."

"Well, I was preoccupied."

"With what?"

"With you. I was so glad you had agreed to come." He inclined closer. "Very glad, Cyn."

Nervously she turned her head away.

"You look beautiful tonight."

"Thank you," she replied huskily. "But will you look at my hair? It's falling—"

"Cyn."

"Down. I can never get it to—"

"Cyn."

"Stay up. Bobby pins slide right—"

He ducked his head and kissed the lobe of her ear, then behind it. He glanced the corner of her lips with his, touching them briefly, experimentally. His were soft and warm. She wanted to feel the pressure of them against hers. Yearning welled up inside her so strongly she couldn't breathe. A soft explosion of desire left her middle feeling warm and heavy.

But she cautiously angled her head back and gave him a vapid smile. "We'd better get back to the suite, Worth."

He looked deeply into her eyes, smiled regretfully, then nodded. "Okay."

He walked close to her, not quite touching. Though she could feel his eyes on her, she didn't dare meet his gaze. The climb was strenuous, but her heart pounded more than the exercise warranted. She was breathless and dizzy by the time they passed through the gate leading to their suite.

Reaching around her, Worth unlocked the door. She preceded him inside and dropped her evening bag into a chair. She turned to say something, but never remembered what she had intended to say because his hands came up and he touched her.

He removed her hair clamp. The escaping strands spilled over his hands; he sank his fingers into them, drawing her face up beneath his.

His lips settled against hers. She felt the damp sweep of his tongue across them. Uttering a soft whimper, she lifted her hands to his with every intention of removing them from around her face and stepping away. Instead, she covered the backs of his hands with her palms and moved closer. Her breasts were flattened against his chest; their thighs came together; his erection nudged her cleft.

From there it got very wild very fast.

Rubbing her lips apart with his, he angled his head to one side and sent his tongue deep into her mouth. She moaned, with disbelief, with joy, with hunger. His hands moved to her waist and pulled her more firmly against him. He smoothed them over her derriere and held her against the front of his body while he continued to kiss her ravenously.

She clutched at him and responded in kind to the hungry thrusts of his tongue. He released her long enough to pull his shirt from his waistband and rip it open. Kissing her madly, he unbuckled his belt and unfastened his trousers, then gathered her against him again.

He caressed her breast through the insubstantial material of her dress. Dissatisfied with that, he reached behind her neck and undid the snap.

Cyn gave a soft, ecstatic cry when her flushed breasts met the furry, warm solidity of his chest. Worth released a low, tortured groan. Still unwilling for their lips to part, he clumsily worked out of his coat and shirt. His fingers fumbled with the zipper at her waist, but when it was undone, he pushed the dress past her hips until it slid down her thighs to the floor. Putting his arms around her, he lifted her out of the pool of fabric surrounding her feet and carried her to the bed.

They fell on it together. He stretched out on top of her, kissing her frantically as he struggled out of his trousers. Finally free of all his clothing, he paused to look down at her.

Her breasts rose out of the band of pale skin bisecting her tan. He cursed softly as his hands moved over them, lightly grinding the dusky, raised centers with his palms, then bending his head and covering them with kisses before taking her nipple into his mouth.

Her back bowed off the bed. Supporting the small of her back, he lifted her stomach to his descending mouth. He kissed it, kissed her mound through the triangle of silk covering it, then removed that and kissed the tuft of soft hair.

Heartbeats later, he was pulsing inside her. She was tight and small and resistant, until her body stretched to accommodate him. When he was buried completely inside her, he levered himself up and back until he was on his knees and she was astride his lap.

"Make it right for you, Cyn," he whispered roughly as his open mouth whisked her beaded nipples.

Cyn closed her arms around his head, hugging it tightly against her, while she pressed her hips down onto his thighs, sending his steely length to the gate of her womb. Her body gloved his fullness. When he flicked his tongue over the very tip of her breast, her entire being quickened and climaxed.

She was gasping for breath when he eased her back onto the bed. His smile was tender as he brushed tendrils of damp hair off her face and laid them one by one upon the pillow.

Within seconds, however, his expression changed. It became taut with intensity and concentration. He began to move inside her, advancing and retreating with a skill that reawakened the passions she had believed were spent.

When they consumed her the second time, the pleasure was heightened by hearing Worth's hoarse cry and feeling his searing release deep inside her.

Seven

Cyn was already dressed and packed by the time Worth woke up the following morning.

Stiffly seated in a chair, she watched his fingers close around nothingness, which, until a while ago, had been her breast. He groped for her among the tangled covers before he woke up and realized that she was no longer lying within the circle of his arms.

Blinking her into focus as he sat up, he assessed her taut expression and the packed bag at her feet. Already knowing the answer, he asked, "What are you doing?"

"Leaving."

"Right. Tonight."

"Wrong. On the next flight to Dallas."

"Now, Cyn—"

"You can't change my mind, so don't even try."

She left her chair and turned her back on him because he looked so damned sexy with the covers settled around his hips— rumpled, unshaven, drowsy, sitting amidst the sheets that were redolent of their love- making.

"The tickets won't be any good on an earlier flight."

"As soon as I woke up," she told him, "I called the airline and agreed to pay the dif- ference in price if they would change my flight."

"*Your* flight?"

"That's right. You don't have to bother with changing yours. Stay and enjoy the rest of your getaway."

"Not likely." Flinging back the covers, he bore down on her. He caught her arm and spun her around to face his rangy naked- ness. "We're partners in this crime. If you go back early, I go back early."

She wrenched her arm from his clasp. "Fine. Do whatever you want."

After stamping into the bathroom, he slammed the door resoundingly. Cyn heard their breakfast being delivered to the dumb-waiter. The thought of food was revolting, but she sipped a cup of coffee in hostile silence on the terrace while he showered, dressed, and packed his bag.

She overheard him placing a call to the airline, making arrangements for his own flight. When tears began to sting her eyes, she blamed them on the rising tropical sun and its glaring reflection off the panoply of white stucco.

"Ready?" He stood framed in the terrace door. "We've got to leave now or we'll miss the flight."

Resisting the urge to gaze at the gorgeous view one last time, or give the suite a farewell glance, she stoically marched away from it and climbed into the Jeep.

Worth handled the details of checking out and turning in the Jeep. Cyn let him, deciding she would pay him for her half later, at some undetermined point in the future when she could look him in the eye without cringing or bursting into tears, either of which she felt she might do at any moment.

Their taxi ride to the airport was dustier, noisier, and more crowded than the one upon their arrival. They paid their departure tax and waited in the airport lounge with other tired, sunburned, cantankerous tourists, who, now that their vacations were over, seemed eager to argue with somebody in their own language. It seemed a lifetime before the plane was ready to board.

Cyn had hoped that since they'd changed their tickets they wouldn't be sitting together, but obviously Worth had made certain they would be. Taking the window seat, she gazed out sightlessly until they had reached their cruising altitude.

Unlike the flight down to Acapulco, which had had a party atmosphere, the passengers on the return trip were quiet and subdued when not downright surly. Most fell asleep as soon as the Continental breakfast was served.

Worth propped his elbow on the armrest between them and leaned toward her. "Cyn, aren't you ever going to speak to me again?"

"Of course. Don't be silly," she replied,

addressing the clouds outside the aircraft's window.

"Are you ever going to look at me again?"

She did, instantly resenting his grin and attempted levity. "I can look at you, but I probably won't be able to face myself in the mirror."

"Why? Because you went to bed with me?"

"Shh! Why don't you just borrow the captain's microphone and announce it to everybody?" She glanced around uneasily, but as far as she could tell, no one had overheard. She whispered, "I don't want to talk about what happened last night."

"I do."

"Then you'll be talking to yourself, because I won't be listening." She turned her head away.

Several minutes elapsed. She had thought—hoped—that he had heeded her wish. Then his low voice spoke directly into her ear. "You wanted it to happen as much as I did, Cyn." Making a small injured sound, she looked at him again. "Who are you mad at?" he asked quietly. "Yourself, for enjoying it? Or me, for making you enjoy it?"

"I didn't enjoy it!"

That made him mad. "The hell you didn't," he snapped close to her face. "You weren't faking it, and I damn sure wasn't. Lie to yourself if it makes you feel better, but that's what it'll be—a lie. You nearly wrung the life out of me, twice, so don't pretend now that you weren't having a good time."

Her cheeks turned scarlet. "What I meant was that I didn't enjoy it afterward."

"Oh, I see," he said, each word laced with sarcasm, "you didn't enjoy lying curled up with me all night, your bottom tucked against my groin and my hand on your breast."

She raised cold, damp hands to her flaming dry cheeks. Her memories were vivid of the times during the night when she had awakened to his fingertips feathering her nipple. Each time, she had purred and stretched against him before falling back to sleep. He was a real cad to remind her how wantonly she had welcomed his caresses.

"In the light of day," she said tightly, "I realize how recklessly I behaved. I'm not casting all the blame on you. Although you have far greater experience in . . . in . . ."

"Pleasures of the flesh?"

"Pleasures" didn't even come close to

describing the responses he'd coaxed from her flesh. Frowning at her own mutinous thought, she doggedly continued. "We fell victim to the circumstances and the climate and the romantic ambience of the place. That's all." As primly as a schoolmarm, she added, "I just want to forget it."

"Fine."

"Good."

"We'll forget it."

"Okay. That's what I just said."

She opened the American magazine she'd bought in the airport before they left. To her relief, Worth rested his head on the back of his seat and closed his eyes. Several minutes passed while she pretended to absorb the printed words in front of her and he pretended to doze.

Finally he rolled his head toward her. "Cyn?"

"Hmm?"

"I don't think I'll ever forget it."

Miserably she caught her forehead on the heel of her hand.

He touched her knee consolingly. "It was just too damn good."

"Was it?"

Before she realized what she was going

to do or say, her head had popped up and she'd asked the question. If she were baldly honest with herself, she would have to admit that much of her anger stemmed from insecurity. Worth had slept with dozens of women, scores of women, women younger and prettier and sexier than she. She was haunted by how she had compared.

"Hell yes it was good. It was fantastic." Then he composed his features and gave a small indifferent shrug. "I thought so, anyway. Did, uh, did you?"

Unable to look at him, she closed her eyes and nodded.

If she hadn't been so steeped in her own insecurity, she would have noticed the trace of it in Worth's voice. "Of course, Tim is the only man you can compare me to."

Catching her lower lip between her teeth, she shook her head adamantly and said, "Don't mention Tim."

"I know how you feel, Cyn," he said on a heavy sigh. "Do you think I'm so insensitive that I don't feel guilty as hell for sleeping with his wife?"

"Widow."

"Right!" he exclaimed in a stage whisper. "His *widow*. His widow of two years. In all that time, in all the time you were married to him, I never had a single licentious thought about you. I swear."

"I know that."

"So why do I feel so damn guilty over last night?" he asked rhetorically. "I wasn't thinking about Tim when I was sitting across the dinner table from you, watching your expressions change in the candlelight, and wishing I could feel your hair on my skin, and wanting to kiss your mouth while you were devouring that creamy dessert."

"Don't, Worth."

Unmindful of her misery, he leaned toward her and lowered his voice another decibel. "Cyn, when your mouth opened beneath mine, when I touched your breasts, you were the only one on my mind. Not Tim, not anybody. You were so warm and sweet, so—"

"Hush, please."

"I couldn't have stopped myself from getting inside you if Tim had walked through the door."

She covered her ears with her hands. He pulled them down. "We might have to readjust our thinking about some things, but we've got nothing to feel guilty about."

"Nothing?" she asked thinly. "Worth, it frightens me that I responded with such abandon. I've never done anything like that before."

"I know."

"I was so totally out of—"

It was like crashing into a concrete wall going a hundred miles an hour. That's how suddenly her words broke off and her emotionality vanished. For several moments she didn't even breathe, but only stared at him blankly. "What did you say?"

"When?"

"Just now. You said, 'I know,' when I told you I'd never behaved like that before."

"Oh, that." He began fidgeting in his seat and cleared his throat uncomfortably. "I just meant that . . . you know, that you don't sleep around."

She continued staring at him with growing distrust. "Did Tim ever confide in you about our personal life?"

"No. Say, would you like something to drink? I'll signal the—"

Cyn curled her fingers around his lower arm. "Did Tim ever confide in you about our personal life?"

"We were best friends, Cyn," he said

plaintively. "You know how guys spout off. They get together, have a few beers, the subject turns to women, and they start saying things they don't really mean."

Tears sprang into her eyes, but fury, not sorrow, was at their source. "Was Tim dissatisfied with me in bed? Did he tell you that?"

"No."

"Worth!"

He gnawed on his lower lip. "Okay, maybe he did drop a few hints to that effect. What husband, at one time or another, doesn't wish his wife were more creative in bed?"

She swallowed several times to keep her nausea down. Her chest felt as though it was breaking up, caving in upon itself. "Tim was disappointed with our sex life?"

Worth mumbled a string of oaths. "Did I say that? No. All I said was that Tim—and I think it was soon after Brandon was born—remarked that your love life wasn't as exciting as it could be, that you didn't warm up to him like—"

"He said I was cold?"

"Not cold," he argued irritably. "Don't put words in my mouth, Cyn. Tim was just belly-aching because things had gotten a little stale. 'Routine' was the word I think he used.

"I told him he was partially to blame," he continued. "See, after their wives have babies, some men start seeing them as maternal creatures instead of sexual creatures. I advised Tim to start treating you like a mistress and you'd start acting like one."

Cyn was trembling with wrath. "You know all the answers where women are concerned, don't you, Worth?"

"What's that supposed to mean?"

"You wanted to see for yourself if I was a sexual creature. You took me to bed just so you'd know firsthand how disappointing my performance was."

His earlier swear words paled in comparison to the ones he now repeated beneath his breath, while his fists clenched reflexively and his eyes blinked furiously.

"You know that's crap, Cyn. Dammit, you know better."

"Excuse me. I'm going to the rest room."

She clambered over his feet and stumbled into the aisle. In the rest room, she was sick. She stayed locked inside the cubicle long after she had emptied her stomach, her ears roaring louder than the jet engine mounted in the tail of the aircraft.

While bathing her face in cold water, she wished she could see Tim alone for five minutes so she could vent her anger on him. How dared he discuss their sex life with Worth? *Worth,* of all people. The ladies' man. The playboy. The man-about-town.

What kind of advice had Tim expected to hear from a single swinger about a marital concern? If he had had something to say on the subject, why hadn't he come to her? She'd been disgustingly content with their sex life and couldn't feel more betrayed if she had learned that Tim had had an extra-marital affair.

But Tim's transgression was nothing compared to Worth's. He had exploited the information his late friend had confided in him. She hadn't known a man, any man, could stoop that low. The only thing she couldn't figure out was why it had taken him so long to appease his curiosity.

Once she returned to her seat, she refused to speak to him. The flight to Dallas seemed to take three times as long as the flight to Acapulco had, but finally the plane landed and they began to disembark.

She slipped past the other tourists, dodging spangled sombreros and gaudy piñatas. Since she didn't have any luggage to claim at the carousel, she was one of the first in line to clear customs. Unfortunately, so was Worth. He got in line directly behind her.

"You've jumped to the wrong conclusion, Cyn. Tim mentioned it one time, I swear. You'd probably just had a fight or something. No big deal. I hadn't even thought about that conversation until you brought it up."

"I'll bet," she said, speaking over her shoulder and keeping her back to him.

"It's the truth. I sure as hell wasn't thinking about it last night."

She spun around to confront him. "You lured me down to Acapulco—"

"I didn't *lure* you to do anything."

"Because I was one of the few women you hadn't been to bed with, right?"

"Wrong."

"You took advantage of my blues and talked me into going with you because you had to see for yourself if Tim's widow was as cold and noncreative in bed as he had said."

Getting angry in his own right, Worth said, "From what I could tell, he had no room for complaint. Not if you rode him as hard as you did me."

She gasped softly and shuddered, but more from ecstatic recollection than shame. In a quaking voice she said, "If you happened to coax a warm response out of me—"

"Warm! That's a hoot. Fiery, maybe. Hot, certainly. But a damn sight higher than 'warm.' "

"If you got any response from me at all, you could privately gloat over it, knowing you had bested your best friend in the only contest between men that really counts."

"Next!" the customs officer called. Cyn moved toward the counter.

"Cyn, wait." Worth stepped across the yellow line.

An official intercepted him. "It's not your turn, sir."

"I'm with that lady."

"Is she your wife?"

"No."

"Wait your turn."

"Damn."

"What was the purpose of your trip to

Mexico, Mrs. McCall?" the official behind the counter asked her as he opened her passport.

"Vacation."

"Anything to declare?"

"Cyn!" Worth shouted.

"Two silver bracelets and a bullwhip."

The official stamped her reentry card. "Thank you."

She gathered her belongings and headed for the escalator.

Worth rushed forward to take her place. "I went to Mexico for a vacation and I didn't buy anything."

The official studied his passport. "Let's take a look inside your bag, please."

"But—" Worth glanced around. The escalator was conveying Cyn up and out of sight.

"Open your bag, please, Mr. Lansing."

Thoroughly disgusted with the denouement of the weekend, Worth unzipped his bag.

Cyn paid the cabdriver at the curb in front of her house. The Sunday newspapers were still lying in the driveway, which was unusual because Ladonia always read them over her morning coffee.

Curious, Cyn picked them up and followed the driveway around to the back of the house. The kitchen door was locked, but Cyn could see her mother standing at the range, turning bacon in a skillet. She tapped on the window. Ladonia glanced over her shoulder and, when she saw Cyn standing on the steps, registered surprise. Removing the skillet from the burner, she hastened to open the door.

"Cyn, what in the world—"

"It's a long story, Mother." Tiredly she dumped everything she was carrying onto one of the kitchen chairs.

"I didn't think you were due back until this evening."

"We weren't originally. We decided to come back early."

"Where's Worth? How'd you get home? Why did you decide to cut your trip short?"

Cyn already had a pounding headache. The questions were bouncing against it like bowling balls. Massaging her temples, she asked, "Why are you having breakfast in the dining room?"

She'd noticed through the connecting

archway that the table was set with a centerpiece of fresh flowers, linen napkins, and
the good china. Delicious aromas were
wafting from the oven, but the thought of
food made her stomach queasy again.

"Cynthia, are you ill? Why'd you come
back early?"

"It was a spur-of-the-moment decision."

"Were the accommodations not up to
par?"

"Actually, the resort exceeded my expectations."

"Sunburn?"

"I used a sunscreen."

"Montezuma's revenge?"

"No."

"Then I don't understand."

"We just got tired of it, that's all," she said
shortly.

"Why?"

"Where's Brandon?"

"Where's Worth?"

The rhythm of their argument was giving
her motion sickness. "Worth and I separated at the airport. I took a cab." She
moved toward the door that led into the rest
of the house. "I'm going to check on Brandon, then shower and go to bed. We had to

get up awfully early to catch the flight. I'll explain everything later."

She was still several steps from the door when a man suddenly appeared, blocking her path, wearing a cheerful smile and a striped bathrobe. As they confronted each other, it would be tough to gauge who was the more shocked.

"Cyn," Ladonia said pleasantly, "I believe you know our neighbor, Mr. Tanton."

Eight

Naturally Cyn knew Mr. Tanton. He had lived two houses down from her since Tim and she had bought this house. His lawn was the envy of the neighborhood, which was known for the conscientious landscaping of the homeowners. Being retired, Charlie Tanton spent hours cultivating his flowerbeds and keeping his grass, trees, and shrubs perfectly manicured.

He was friendly, neighborly, and a soft touch for any schoolkid peddling fund-raising candy or raffle tickets. He was soft-spoken, kind, and conservative . . . and the last person Cyn would have expected to find in his bathrobe, in her kitchen, late on a Sunday morning.

"Charlie, are you ready for coffee?" Ladonia, the only one of the three who remained unruffled, poured him a cup, and sidestepped her astonished daughter to hand it to him. She gave his arm a reassuring pat. "Brunch is almost ready. You don't mind if Cyn joins us, do you? She returned early from—"

"Excuse me." Cyn bolted past her neighbor, who appeared to be as disconcerted as she. She ran first for Brandon's bedroom. His bed was made, but he was nowhere in sight.

Ladonia caught up with her seconds after she entered the bedroom she had shared with Tim, although she'd heeded advice and redecorated it soon after his death.

As soon as Ladonia closed the door, Cyn confronted her. "Where is Brandon?"

"He was invited to sleep over with Shane Lattimore last night. Today, after Sunday school, they're going to the zoo."

"So you were free to invite your *boyfriend* over to spend the night."

"Exactly," Ladonia replied with admirable equanimity.

At fifty-one, Ladonia Patterson was a stunning woman. Her hair was the same caramel shade as her daughter's, but she had kept it artfully frosted for years to camouflage any gray. Her eyes were the color of sherry. She was slender and could have passed for a woman ten years younger. Pragmatism was her middle name, so it was characteristic of her not to mince words.

"Charlie and I have been wanting to spend the night with each other for months. Last night was the first opportunity we've had."

Cyn's knees buckled. She dropped to the edge of her bed, stupefied by her mother's brazen admission.

"I don't understand why you're so upset, Cynthia. It was my party that was spoiled by your unannounced arrival."

"How . . . how long has this been going on?"

"Let's see." Ladonia tilted her head to an angle of concentration. "Since last spring, when Charlie brought me a beautiful bouquet of tulips from his flowerbeds. I invited him in for coffee and he stayed over an hour."

She touched her cheek, which a girlish

blush had turned pink. "We'd been doing silly things like inventing reasons to stroll past the other's house. We seemed to go out for the mail at the same time every day, which gave us an excuse to speak to each other. He borrowed so many cups of sugar, I accused him of having a still. The day after he brought the tulips, he invited me out to lunch. That was our first official date."

"Where was I? Where was Brandon?"

"You were at work and Brandon went with us." She frowned at Cyn's incredulous expression. "For goodness' sake, Cynthia, it's been a very proper courtship. Don't be such a prude. We didn't make love until last night, certainly never when Brandon was in the house."

"You're having an affair with Charlie Tanton?"

"That's a tacky word to pin on what we feel for each other. I can't say I like your censorious expression or tone of voice either. I'm single. So is Charlie. His wife died seven years ago. We share many common interests and have a wonderful time together." Her eyes sparkled. "He's very sexy, don't you think?"

Cyn was at a loss for words.

"Last night confirmed that we're compatible in *everything,* so we decided to make it official."

"You're moving in with him?"

"Of course not," Ladonia retorted with affront. "We're getting married."

"Married?"

"Yes! Isn't that wonderful?"

"Married? When?"

"As soon as arrangements can be made."

Cyn left the bed and moved to the window. She pushed aside the shutters and gazed out, but nothing her eyes took in registered with her. "Just like that?" she asked, turning to address her mother again.

"Oh, dear. Charlie was worried about how you'd take the news, but I pooh-poohed his concern. I'm disappointed in you. I didn't think you'd be one of those children who have difficulty accepting stepparents."

"Don't be ridiculous."

"Then what's the matter with you? Why aren't you happy for me?"

Cyn spread her arms away from her body in a gesture of helplessness. "It's so unexpected, Mother. So sudden."

"We've been dating for months."

"On the sly. Sneaking around while I was at work. Did you bribe Brandon to keep quiet about your little tête-à-tête? Why didn't you ever tell me? Why did you keep it a secret?" She laughed scoffingly. "Did you expect me to just look through him when he showed up in our kitchen in his bathrobe, as though that were an everyday occurrence?"

"I can see that you're in no mood to discuss this now. Furthermore, I won't let you spoil this day for me." She turned to go.

"Mother! Why am I the last to know?"

Ladonia came back around, but her chin was elevated with hauteur. "All right, Cynthia, since you asked, I'll tell you why I kept my romance a secret from you. I felt badly because I had a new life and you didn't."

"What?"

"That's it in a nutshell. I was widowed six months after you, but I recovered much faster. I urged you to get on with your life. So did Worth. So did everyone who cared about you. You, however, never seized the initiative. All you did was mope around and complain about how boring and dull and dissatisfying everything was. You seemed determined to feel sorry for yourself."

Ladonia drew herself up even straighter.

"Well, I wasn't. Charlie came into my life like a breath of fresh air. I loved your father with all my heart. You know I did. Charlie knows I did too, just like I know he loved his Kate. Because our lives were so rich and fulfilled before we met, we can bring even more love and happiness to each other now.

"There are scores of women my age, and many much younger, who would love to snatch up Charlie." Her eyes glowed with what was unmistakably love and joy. Cyn marveled that she hadn't noticed her mother's buoyancy before.

"Charlie thinks I'm cute and funny and, as of last night, terrific in bed. So, about four o'clock this morning when he proposed, I said yes. And frankly, Cynthia, I didn't even think of you when I gave him my answer. If you don't like it, that's just too damn bad."

Turning, she made a sweeping exit befitting a grande dame of the theater.

Cyn stared at the closed door until her pounding headache propelled her into the bathroom, where she took two aspirin tablets and filled the tub with hot water. After soaking for half an hour, long enough for the aspirin to dull her headache, she dressed.

Opting for togetherness rather than the automatic dishwasher, Ladonia and Charlie were doing the dishes when Cyn entered the kitchen unseen. Ladonia was washing; Charlie was drying. They were laughing at an in-joke. Cyn felt a sharp pang of envy, and hated herself for feeling it.

"Mother, Mr. Tanton." Surprised by the sound of her voice, they turned. Cyn clasped her hands together nervously. "I . . . I want you to . . . Congratulations," she finished lamely.

"Thank you, dear," Ladonia said graciously, as though their previous argument had never taken place.

"Along with my congratulations, please accept my apology for the way I behaved earlier." She fashioned a stiff little smile. "You took me by surprise."

"Apology accepted," Ladonia said swiftly, noticing the tears that had clouded her daughter's eyes. "Would you like some coffee? It's still hot. Or maybe tea would be better. You look pale despite your new tan."

"Tea sounds good."

Charlie laid his dish towel aside and moved toward Cyn. Even though he was dressed now, he couldn't quite meet her eyes and tugged on his earlobe self-consciously.

"You must have got the wrong idea earlier, and I can't blame you if you did." He raised his gentle eyes and looked at her fully, though his face was still ruddy with embarrassment. "I want you to know that I respect your mother, Mrs. McCall. I wouldn't have done, nor do I plan to do, anything that would jeopardize her happiness or hurt her in any way."

Cyn laid her hand on his arm. "I overreacted, which is a character flaw of mine. Now that I've had time to adjust to the news, I'm delighted. Mother deserves to be happy. I believe you've made her awfully happy."

His smile conveyed profound relief. "Good. Well, that's very good," he blustered. "Please call me Charlie from now on."

"I'm Cynthia or Cyn." Clasping hands, they smiled at each other warmly.

As a peace offering, she presented her mother with the Mexican silver bracelet. Ladonia loved it, as Cyn had known she would. While Cyn drank her cup of tea and nibbled at a leftover blueberry muffin, they discussed the wedding plans. The couple planned to hold a small, intimate ceremony at Ladonia and Cyn's house, with only their immediate families and the minister attending.

The prospective bride and groom soon left together, saying they were going to watch a football game at Charlie's house. Watching them walk arm in arm down the sidewalk, their progress imperiled because they couldn't keep their eyes off each other, Cyn figured that there would be some heavy necking going on during the game.

Again she felt a twinge of emotion around her heart that was more yearning than envy. She didn't wish their happiness away from them, but was jealous of their wholeness, which came from being one of two instead of one alone.

Brandon was deposited at home by his playmate's parents in the middle of the afternoon. He was excited to see his mother, but just as excited about his recent trip to the zoo. The bullwhip she'd brought him was a success.

"I like it almost as much as the guns Worth gave me," he chirped as he bolted through the door on his way outside to try it out.

Simply hearing Worth's name made her insides clench with a mix of desire and disappointment.

Ladonia returned home in time for supper. They ate from TV trays in the den while watching a Disney show with Brandon. The telephone rang midway through the program. Ladonia got up to answer.

"It's probably Charlie. He said he'd call after he notified his children of our plans."

She was gone for several minutes. Cyn could hear her laughing. When she reappeared, she said, "It's for you."

"Me? Who is it?"

"Worth. I swear that man is crazy. When I told him I was getting married, he pretended to break down and cry."

"I don't want to talk to him."

Ladonia's lingering laughter vanished. "Why not?"

"I still have a slight headache and just don't feel up to it." She tried to sound casual, but knew she hadn't fooled her perceptive mother.

"That's not very polite, Cynthia."

"I'm sorry. I don't want to talk right now. I haven't been with Brandon for days."

Brandon couldn't have cared less. He

was totally absorbed in the adventure tale about a family taking a river-raft trip.

Ladonia, crossing her arms over her middle, struck a pose of parental inquisition that demanded the truth. "What happened between you and Worth in Acapulco?"

"Nothing!" Cyn exclaimed. "I just don't want to talk right now."

"What'll I tell him?"

"Tell him I'm not feeling well. No, wait, tell him I'm tired since I didn't get much sleep last night. No, no, don't say that. Tell him I'm going out."

"Well, which is it?"

"Tell him I'm going out."

"I won't lie for you."

"Then tell him I'm busy and can't come to the phone. If he's got any manners at all, he won't press you for an explanation."

Cyn was on the receiving end of a reproachful look, but Ladonia did as she asked. Charlie called shortly after that. Ladonia stayed on the phone with him for hours, billing and cooing, apparently making up for all the time they'd kept their budding romance a secret.

Once Brandon was in bed, his prayers said and good-night kisses dispensed, Cyn went gratefully into her own room. She still had to face the task of unpacking. Each item she removed from her bag reminded her in some particular way of Worth and their weekend together.

He had complimented her on this blouse, saying the color made her skin luminescent. He had stroked her cheek.

He'd said her legs looked especially terrific in these shorts. He had squeezed her calf.

These sandals made her toes look sexy and "damn near edible." He had brushed his fingertips across her toes.

"Flattery," she muttered, stoking the smoldering fire of her fury. Ruefully she added, "But it got him what he wanted, didn't it?"

Stronger than her resentment, however, was her heartache. Her eyes filled with bitter tears when she unpacked the dress he had urged her to buy, complimented her on, then removed from her body with such passion-driven haste.

Once in her own familiar bed, she tried comforting herself with memories of loving Tim. Sure, she conceded, there had been times when she probably could have exercised more initiative.

There had also been times when he could have. He hadn't hit the mark one hundred percent of the time, but you didn't hear her complaining, did you? She hadn't always been fulfilled. The earth hadn't always moved. The stars hadn't always showered her with fire.

Certainly never anything like last night.

As quickly as her mind conjured up that disloyal thought, she qualified it. Her extraordinary surge of passion had been justified. It had been a long time since she'd been with a man, that's all. Just think how much desire a healthy young woman could store up in two years' time. No wonder her response to the first man who touched her had been so explosive.

But she doubted that was entirely true. Since Tim's death, other men had tried to tap into her sexuality, most recently Josh Masters. She hadn't liquefied in his arms.

"Damn you, Worth Lansing," she whispered into her pillow as, with a low moan, she rolled to her side and drew her knees toward her chest.

Even as she cursed him, she longed to

feel his strong arms bridging her body, his hands cupping her hips, holding them poised for his hard, smooth penetration. The recollections of his kisses were vivid. Closing her eyes, she could feel again the tugging pressure of his lips on her breasts and the ardent, damp flicking of his tongue against her skin.

Never again would she experience that wild, fierce brand of lovemaking. Not only had he caused her to respond shamefully, he had ruined other men for her. Even Tim, whose lovemaking had been tender or passionate, as the mood called for, paled in comparison to Worth.

He had injured her in three ways. First by coaxing her body to betray her, then by making her angry at her late husband, who wasn't even there to defend himself, and finally by robbing her of her best friend. She felt that loss almost as grievously as she felt used.

In the darkest part of her soul she hoped Worth was as miserable as she, but he was probably celebrating. He'd accomplished what he'd set out to do.

*   *   *

"I asked for a diet drink." Worth frowned into the glass of soda the long-suffering Mrs. Hardiman had just poured for him.

"That's what you got." By Thursday of that week, even her patience was wearing thin with his constant griping.

"It doesn't taste like diet soda."

"Well, that's what it is," she said with mounting asperity. "You've been impossible to please all week. What's wrong with you?"

"Nothing." Broodingly he bobbed a floating ice cube up and down with his fingertip.

"I thought you'd be pleased with the handsome commissions you've earned this week."

He shrugged, but said nothing.

"You even got that fat portfolio."

"I had to court the old broad long enough," he grumbled.

"She thinks you're simply adorable. She told me so when she stopped by yesterday afternoon. But then, she hasn't had to put up with your behavior this week like I have." Mrs. Hardiman passed him a coaster for his drink. "Something's wrong. Is it your love life?"

"Hell no!" he exclaimed, correcting his

slouching posture in his desk chair. "My love life's fine, thank you."

She regarded him skeptically. "I thought the trip to Mexico would do you good."

"Well, it didn't."

"Greta has called twice today. She no longer believes me when I tell her you're either out or on another line. I'm running out of excuses."

"Part of your salary goes to making up excuses for me."

Mrs. Hardiman took another tack. "I think Greta's feelings are hurt because you haven't returned her calls."

"Tough." He wasn't quite ready to forgive her for standing him up at the last minute. Look what had happened as a result. He had lost his best friend.

So what if Greta was upset because he was avoiding her? Why should he be the only sucker in town whose calls weren't returned? Since Sunday night he had made about a dozen a day that had gone unacknowledged.

"Well, either cheer up or fire me," Mrs. Hardiman said as she retrieved the correspondence she had brought in for his signature.

"If you don't like the working conditions around here," he said crossly, "why don't you just quit?"

At the door, she turned and gave him the regal, condescending stare usually reserved for recalcitrant clients and ill-mannered deliverymen. "I don't have the heart. I never kick a man when he's down."

"Women!" Worth mouthed after she had slammed out. Whatever their capacity in your life, they gave you hell.

He left his desk and putted a few golf balls toward the cup. He blamed the three straight misses on an imaginary ripple in the carpet. Slinging aside the putter, he kicked his basketball out of his path. None of his toys had helped elevate his mood this week.

Several times he had considered going out, but couldn't think of one woman he wanted to be with enough to put forth the effort of making a date. Nor did he feel like cruising alone to see what he could harvest in one of the nightclubs he frequented.

He'd halfheartedly considered pursuing the lady lawyer who had an office in his building, but the very thought of the chase made him feel tired. Besides, since returning from Mexico he'd run into her several times in the parking garage and had decided that her legs weren't all that spectacular. Her nose was too long and her lips were too thin and her hair was too curly. Her eyes weren't merely cunning, but devious.

She didn't have the loose-limbed moves of a colt or a funny little laugh or a habit of wetting her lips before saying something of importance. She wasn't Cyn.

Cyn was the only woman he wanted to see; and she, unfortunately, wasn't speaking to him.

How could she be so mule-headed as to believe that when he'd made love to her he was just trying to see if he could make her burn hotter than Tim had? Of all the asinine, juvenile, female assumptions to make!

If it was so asinine, juvenile, and female, why was he worrying about it? Why didn't he simply chalk it up to the damnable feminine psyche, which, since Eve, had never jibed with logic? He'd always thought Cyn was above that kind of foolishness, but obviously he'd been wrong.

She would eventually come around. They always did.

In the meantime, to hell with this. He'd

had enough of moping. On a sudden burst of resolution, he yanked his suit jacket off the chrome coat tree and stormed through the door of his office.

"Leaving early?" Mrs. Hardiman inquired.

"Going to the gym. Oh, and if Greta calls tomorrow, put her through immediately."

Cyn's heart went out to the girl sitting across the desk from her. She didn't fit the profile of most of the clients who came to the women's hospital for counseling. Ordinarily they came from mid- to lower-income backgrounds. Generally they had little or no parental supervision and had been sexually active since, or even before, puberty.

Sheryl Davenport was the third daughter of a North Dallas real-estate tycoon and his socialite wife. Sheryl's oldest sister was a renowned corporate attorney; the other was married to a peer of the realm, a polo teammate of the Prince of Wales.

The circumstances of Sheryl's predicament were no more tragic than any other, but because of the high public profile her family maintained, the consequences would probably be more catastrophic.

"I just can't kill a baby." Glossy blond hair fell like a curtain over both sides of her face as she sobbed into an embroidered hand-kerchief. "If I told my parents I was preg-nant, I know that's what they would demand that I do. One of my sisters had an abortion, but she was older, already in college, when it happened. No one except the family ever knew. Daddy kept it hushed up."

Sheryl was a straight-A student in her junior year at an exclusive girls' academy. She was bright, beautiful, and terribly trou-bled. "Have you spoken to any of the coun-selors at your school?" Cyn asked gently.

"No! Lord, no. They'd kick me out and Daddy would have a fit. My mother and both my sisters graduated from there."

"What about the father of the child, Sheryl? Does he know?"

"No."

"Why not?"

"He wouldn't care."

"No possibility of marriage?"

She gave a short mirthless laugh and shook her head. "No. I wouldn't want that."

"Oh?"

"We weren't lovers. I mean, I didn't love him."

"Then it wasn't a long-standing relation-ship?" Cyn asked. Sheryl gave a negative shake of her head. "Is that why you didn't take any precautions?"

"Yes," she replied, shoving back her hair. "You don't have to lecture me on how stupid that was. I already know. It was a heat-of-the-moment kind of thing. I'm sure he assumed I was on birth-control pills. He used a condom, but, well," she said, smiling pitifully, "it didn't work.

"He's an assistant tennis coach at our club. A real ladies' man. Not a marriage candidate. Certainly not a good potential parent either." Her lovely Nordic blue eyes leaked another stream of tears. "Mrs. McCall, what am I going to do?"

Cyn clasped her hands on top of her desk. "If you could choose, without taking anything into consideration except your own wishes, what would you want to do, Sheryl?"

"Have the baby," she said with a soft, wistful smile.

"And keep it?" Cyn asked. Sheryl nodded. "Why?"

"Because it would love me. I mean, babies love their mothers no matter what, right?"

The crack in Cyn's heart widened another degree. Sheryl needed unqualified love because she had never received it. "Then perhaps that's what you should do."

"No," the girl said, sniffing. "That's impossible."

For Cyn to encourage Sheryl to keep her baby would be stepping beyond the boundaries of her role. She could only explore the options with her clients.

"If marriage is out of the question," she said, "and you don't want to terminate the pregnancy, and you don't feel that you could rear the child alone, you could have it and then put it up for adoption."

"I'd like that," Sheryl said, leaving her chair. She began pacing the narrow space between the window and Cyn's desk. "If I knew my baby was going to be placed with a couple who loved each other and would love the baby, I'd like that a lot. But my parents would never let me carry the baby to term. That would ruin all the plans they've mapped out for me."

"What about all the plans you've mapped out for yourself?"

Sheryl stopped pacing and looked at her with perplexity. "I don't have any."

"Well, I think you should." Cyn rose and rounded her desk. She laid her hand on Sheryl's shoulder. "I would be happy to be there and act as a buffer when you break the news to your parents. But you don't have to decide what to do today," she added hastily.

Judging by Sheryl's distress at the mention of such an interview, Cyn thought the Davenports must be holy terrors to have instilled that much fear and dread into their youngest daughter.

"There's still time. You just discovered you were pregnant a few days ago. Give yourself a week or two to adjust to the idea and consider your options." She reached for a business card and pressed it into the young woman's damp hand. "In the meantime, call me if you want to ask a question or just talk. All right?"

With a discouraged sigh, Sheryl nodded. "Okay. Thank you for listening."

"It'll work out for the best. You'll see."

Sheryl looked doubtful of that as she said good-bye and left Cyn's office. Cyn wearily returned to the chair behind her desk and propped her head in her hands. It was Thursday of possibly the worst week she'd had since Tim's death.

All her cases that week had been especially difficult. Or maybe she was in a poor frame of mind to deal with them. The platitudes she'd offered the troubled young women had sounded more banal than usual . . . and grossly hypocritical.

How could she advise them to use caution and common sense in sexual matters when she had exercised none whatsoever before going to bed with Worth? It had been a "heat-of-the-moment kind of thing." That was no excuse.

"Mrs. McCall?"

Wearily she depressed the button on her intercom. "Yes?" She had thought Sheryl Davenport was her last appointment of the day.

"Dr. Masters is here to see you."

Inwardly she groaned, but couldn't think of a gracious way to avoid seeing him. "Send him in."

"Well, hello." He breezed in, looking handsome in his white lab coat.

"Hi, Josh. How are you?"

"I'm fine." He sat down on the corner of

her desk, effectively trapping her behind it. "But you look a little the worse for wear."

"It's been one of those weeks."

"I thought last week was."

"Last week too."

"I called you on Saturday. Your mother said you'd taken a short vacation."

"Yes, well, I did, but it didn't do much good, I'm afraid."

"You haven't returned my calls."

Above all things, she hated being placed in a defensive position, something Josh seemed particularly adroit at creating. "The last time I saw you, we had an argument, remember?"

"I remember. It was over your sex life. Or rather the lack thereof."

Her chin went up a notch. Frostily she asked, "How do you know there's a lack thereof?"

Watching his ingratiating smile collapse made her feel marginally better. Standing, she went around him and reached for her handbag. "I was on my way out." She switched out the light in her office and held open the door.

"Uh, sure, coming." He followed her through the anteroom and into the corridor.

By then he had regained his composure. He slid his hand beneath her arm. "So have you forgiven me enough to have dinner?"

She'd rather have bamboo shoots shoved under her fingernails than spend an evening with just the three of them: herself, the doctor, and his colossal ego.

"I'd love to," she replied, flashing Josh a radiant smile. "When?"

Damned if she was going to let super-stud Worth Lansing think she was a sexual charity case.

Nine

He was at her house when she got home. She recognized the sports car a block away and emitted a scathing, unladylike curse. Couldn't he take a hint? If she had wanted to talk to him, she would have taken his calls.

It rankled even more that he was having a jolly good time with Brandon on the den floor when she entered the room, slinging her purse and briefcase into a chair and assessing the domestic scene with a scowl instead of a smile.

"Hey, Mom, Worth's here!"

"So I see."

Worth was sprawled on his stomach on the carpet. Brandon was straddling the small of his back and beating him about the head and shoulders with a Nerf baseball bat.

"I hope you've come to rescue me," he said to her over his shoulder. He managed to roll over, grasp the boy around the waist, and lift him up, so that Brandon's arms and legs dangled above him. Brandon whooped with glee. Worth's face turned red with exertion.

Through clenched teeth he gasped, "Lord, you're getting heavy. When you were a baby, I could hoist you up like this and keep you there for hours."

He lowered the boy to the floor and, much to Brandon's delight, made a production of struggling into a sitting position and regaining his breath.

"Do it again, Worth. Or lift me up by my heels and hold me upside down."

"Leave him alone, Brandon. He's tired." Cyn detested her waspish tone of voice. It instantly dispelled their cheerfulness. Brandon gazed up at her with hurt and confusion showing on his small face.

"Maybe later," Worth said, ruffling the

boy's hair. "Give me a hand up." Brandon took his hand and hauled him to his feet. "Hi," he said to Cyn, stuffing in his shirttail, which had come out during his scuffle with Brandon.

"Hello."

"How are you?"

"Fine. You?"

"Fine."

"Where's my mother?"

"She went to get Charlie so I could be introduced properly."

"Oh."

Much as she wanted to avoid looking at him, she couldn't seem to drag her eyes away. He must have just come from his health club, because he was dressed in an old pair of jeans, a faded polo shirt, and ancient Docksides with no socks. His hair was disheveled, as though he'd driven his car with the windows open.

It seemed imperative that she avoid looking directly into his eyes, but she was powerless to resist his gaze. His eyes bore into hers like truth-seeking blue lasers.

Their long gaze was finally interrupted by the appearance of Ladonia, who proudly ushered in her intended. As introductions were made, the two men shook hands.

"Charlie, this is breaking my heart, you know," Worth said with a theatrical sigh. "I've been after this woman for years."

Ladonia affectionately patted his cheek. "I'm sorry, Worth. He was just too sexy to resist."

Her statement caused Charlie to blush and Worth to laugh and Cyn to wish that she felt like laughing too. The best she could do was force a smile.

Ladonia said, "Charlie wants to take me out tonight to repay me for the nights he's had dinner here." He'd been a regular at dinner since they'd broken their news to Cyn. "Now that Worth's here, you and Brandon won't have to eat alone."

"I'm sure Worth has other plans, Mother."

"In fact, I came by to see if I could buy everybody a burger. How 'bout it, Ladonia? Charlie?"

"Whatever Ladonia wants to do is fine with me," Charlie said affably.

Ladonia linked her arm through his. "I'd rather be alone with my fiancé if it's all the same to you, Worth."

He gave her a lascivious wink. "You wanton hussy, you. Damn, I wished I'd snagged you when I had the chance." He caught her up into a bear hug.

Several minutes later, the lovebirds left. Cyn turned to Worth and said awkwardly, "Don't feel obligated to take us out."

"I want to. That's what I came for."

"Under the circumstances, Worth—"

"What circumstances?" His innocently posed question was most provoking and set her teeth on edge. Was he going to make her spell it out for him all over again? "Brandon, is McDonald's all right with you?"

"Cheap trick," she said out the side of her mouth as Brandon raced out the front door toward Worth's car.

"But effective," he said, flashing her his most disarming smile. "After you, Mrs. McCall."

"Can I go to the playground now?"

"It's *may* I go, Brandon, and let me check your face first." Cyn made a fleeting swipe across his mouth with a paper napkin before he scooted from his chair and charged for the door leading outside to the playground. "Be careful on the slide," she called. The futility of cautioning him made her sigh.

"Coffee?" Worth removed the plastic tops off the Styrofoam cups.

"Thanks."

For several moments they sipped their coffee while watching Brandon play. He and a little girl about his age arrived at the foot of the slide at the same time. Brandon chivalrously stood aside and let her climb the rungs first.

"A ladies' man in the making," Worth said around a chuckle.

"I hope not."

His gaze swung away from the plate-glass window. He contemplated Cyn's un-smiling face for a moment, then said with undisguised anger, "You know, Cyn, sleep-ing together usually brings people closer to-gether, not wedges them apart."

His superior inflection infuriated her. "That all depends on why they slept to-gether. We know why you slept with me, don't we?"

"Okay, I admit it. I'm slime. Pond scum. The lowest form of life on the whole friggin' planet. There, are you happy?" The orange-

and-yellow chair caught the middle of his back when he flopped back against it, clearly agitated.

"I trucked you off to Mexico just so I could answer a question that had been bugging me for years, that question being what my best friend's wife was like in bed."

He slapped his thighs and blew out a gust of air as he turned his head away. Shortly, however, he sat up and leaned his forearms on the table. "Now that we've settled on why I went to bed with you, why did you go to bed with me?"

"What?"

"Let's hear it. What compelled you?"

"I—"

"One could speculate that you were curious about my sexual performance too."

"I never—"

"Oh, really? Never? Not once? You *never* listened to Tim expound on my sexual exploits and wondered if I was as good as I claimed to be? Didn't you want to test my prowess for yourself?"

"You're disgusting." She reached for her purse and slung the strap over her shoulder.

Before she could slide from her chair, Worth reached across the empty burger boxes and shake cups and grabbed her arm. "See how much that accusation hurts?" His gentle tone arrested her more than his grip on her arm. She resumed her seat and lowered the shoulder strap of her purse. For moments their gazes held. Cyn was the first to lower her eyes.

"It does hurt, doesn't it?"

He nodded slowly. "Very much."

Propping her elbows on the littered table, she caught her face in her hands. "Oh, Worth, I'm sorry," she said. "I don't know what got into me."

His laugh brought her head up. "Shouldn't you rephrase that?"

Coloring, she ducked her head again. "I shouldn't have put all the blame on you. I was looking for a scapegoat. Blaming you relieved my own conscience."

"Conscience? Was what we did so terrible?"

"I felt guilty about it, yes."

"Why, Cyn?"

"Tim, naturally."

"Tim's dead. A more-than-adequate period of mourning has passed. No, it wasn't going to bed with a man that made you feel so guilty. It wasn't even going to bed with

me that made you feel that way." He lowered his voice to an intimate pitch. "What
made you feel so guilty was that you en-
joyed it so much."

She pulled her lower lip through her
teeth.

"Right?"

Miserably she nodded.

"Cyn," he said softly, reaching for her
hand, "Tim wouldn't expect you to remain
celibate. You were only twenty-seven when
he died. Were you supposed to strap on a
chastity belt for the rest of your life?"

"No, but I didn't expect my reinitiation to
be so earth-shattering. I never knew I could
be so uninhibited. I guess I was super-
susceptible."

"The field was fertile, and I, the big bad
wolf, took advantage and plowed it?"

"No," she said, adamantly denying it with
a shake of her head. "You didn't take advantage. I could have prevented it if I'd
really wanted to."

"Thank you for that," he said with a tender smile.

"Recently I've been so discontent. When
an outlet presented itself, I took it without
thinking of the consequences." Wryly she

added, "I wanted something to happen, but I didn't count on it being a one-night stand with you."

He made a face. "You could attach a better name to it, dammit."

"What would you call it?"

"I'm not sure, but nothing as heartless as that. I've had plenty of one-night stands. Believe me, Cyn, what I shared with you didn't start in my groin. It started here," he said, pointing to his head, "and gained momentum here." He dug his index finger into his left pectoral over his heart. "Before it ever moved below my belt."

Her breath staggered on its way out of her lungs. "With me too, Worth."

"Then stop talking nonsense. Don't you know that you mean more to me than an easy lay I picked up in a bar?"

Emotions that had been raw and oozing for days were about to be manifested in tears. Before that happened, she steered the subject to another track, comforted in the knowledge that what had happened hadn't lessened his regard for her.

"Coming on the heels of that, my mother announces that she's getting married."

"You don't want her to? More coffee?"

"No, thanks. Of course I want her to, but it means another shake-up, another period of adjustment." She glanced up at him and frowned. "Sounds selfish, doesn't it?"

"A trifle."

"I hate myself for it."

"Don't. You're human."

"As of last Saturday night, there's no doubt of that, is there?"

Brandon came in to get a drink of water from the fountain, then waved at them and dashed out again.

"He looks like Tim."

"Yes, he does," she conceded with an affectionate smile.

Worth squeezed her hand, which he still held in his. "Cyn, you gotta know that I wasn't thinking about Tim that night." His eyes probed hers, searching for understanding. "If Tim had crossed my mind once, I couldn't have touched you. I would have been thinking of you as his wife, not as a woman who had made me so hard—"

"Worth!"

"It's true. Argue other points if you must, but one thing that is absolutely indisputable is that I wanted you in the most elemental way. And there was physical evidence that you wanted me just as badly. Granted?"

"Granted," she whispered.

"When I held you that night, touched your skin, smelled your hair, kissed your mouth, the only thing on my mind was making love to you. No one else was involved. Just you and me, Cyn. Can't you live with that?"

Nothing could have snapped her out of the trance Worth's sexy earnestness had induced. Nothing except Brandon appearing with two scratched, bloody hands which he'd gotten from landing wrong when he "parachuted" out of the swing.

Ladonia wasn't home yet when they arrived. Worth courageously volunteered to help get Brandon, now tired and cranky, through bathtime and into bed. The boy put up a brave front when Cyn applied antiseptic salve to the injured heels of his hands.

"That macho stiff upper lip was for your benefit," she told Worth as she pulled closed the door to Brandon's bedroom. "If you hadn't been here, he would have—"

He pressed his mouth against hers, giving her another unexpected kiss straight out of left field that she hadn't seen coming or prepared herself for.

He kept it soft and undemanding, allowing her the opportunity to accept or rebuff it. Though she went limp against the wainscoting in the hallway, though it affected her like a punch in the stomach, she didn't let the kiss intensify.

"Don't, Worth."

"What's a kiss between friends?" he whispered against her neck while his fingers strummed the placket of her blouse, gently plucking at the buttons and nudging her breasts with his knuckles.

"Ordinarily, nothing." She moved away from him and headed for better-lighted, more neutral territory in the house.

"So we're extraordinary?"

As she entered the den, she switched on another lamp. "Last Saturday night altered our friendship, Worth. Hasn't that sunk in yet, or are you just being obtuse?"

"You're the one who's being stubborn. You seem to think, now that we've had sex, we can't be friends."

"We can't!"

"How come?"

She threw back her head and ground her

teeth with frustration. "It doesn't work that way, that's how come. It's different now. Everything's changed. It pains me to say it. I regret the loss of our close friendship, but it's irretrievable. We sacrificed it to . . . to . . ."

"To the best damn lovemaking either of us has ever had!" His temper was tenuous at best. "So what's the problem?"

She turned her back on him and fiddled with the pieces of the chess set Charlie and Ladonia had left on the game table. "You're a man and I'm a woman."

"That much I know, Cyn."

"Our respective genders respond differently to situations like this."

He laid his hands on her shoulders and turned her around. "I'm not as dense as you think," he said in a more reasonable tone. "I've ruminated on this for four days. It boils down to this. You don't seem to believe that we can pick up our friendship where it left off."

"That's right," she said tearfully. "I don't."

"Well, you're wrong. We can. We can do anything we set our minds to."

She was shaking her head. "I don't think so, Worth."

"Listen," he said, moving in closer and sending his fingers up through her hair, "I'll promise not to think about it anymore if you will."

"We can't help thoughts that pop into our minds."

"For that very reason it's not officially a sin unless you nurture the thought. So whenever I start remembering how silky your skin feels against mine, I'll just put it out of my mind and start thinking about blue-chip stocks. Or something."

Her expression was dubious, but she wanted desperately to be convinced. "I was sad, thinking that my best friend was no longer available to me."

"So was I."

"Many times this week, I've needed to pick up the phone and call you."

"You're so damned bullheaded."

"But, Worth, I still don't think this is going to work, no matter how good our intentions are."

"Sure it will, if we make up our minds to it. Like tonight, when I found myself gazing at your breasts, all sorts of pictures went through my head. I ignored them. Before long I probably won't even remember how responsive they were to my kisses. And those choppy little sounds you make when you're about to climax," he added huskily. "I can barely hear them in my memory anymore."

She converted her yearning whimper into a cough. Her heartbeat was painfully strong.

"I've had to work at it," he confessed, touching the spot on her throat where her rapid pulse was visible. "It's a matter of self-control."

"I've tried to forget it."

"Any luck?"

"A little."

"But you still remember some of it?"

"Hmm." She nodded as much as his hands would permit her head to move.

"Like what?" he whispered huskily. "Like how it felt to be joined that way? So perfectly . . ." He pressed his forehead against hers. "Ah, Cyn. I remember that part too."

"I think that's the number-one thing we should work on forgetting."

"Right."

He didn't push her away, but he didn't draw her any closer either. After a moment, their breathing returned to normal. "Listen,

Cyn," he said, appealing to her sentimental-
ity, "we've got years of friendship going for
us. That's hard to come by, much harder
than a love affair. We can't sacrifice our for-
mer relationship to one fantastic night in
bed, can we?"

Burying her face in his shirt, she murmured, "Why did we do it?"

"We got caught up in the romantic atmosphere." He rubbed her back consolingly.
"The tropics are like that. They're damned
seductive, and as potent as their drinks that
taste so harmless. Before you know it,
you're drunk on the place." He wrapped his
arms around her. Together their bodies
swayed to music they heard only in their
heads.

"The sea and sun wove a sensual spell
over us, Cyn, along with the unusual circumstances of sharing a room. That combi-
nation sabotaged our senses and got us
naked and into bed together."

"You think so?"

"Must have been. We've never been hot
for each other before."

"We never will be again."

He seemed less inclined to agree to
that, and merely nodded. "We'll only suffer

far-reaching consequences if we let our friendship be affected. It's not like we're strangers, potential health risks to each other. You're not going to get pregnant."

Suddenly he took her by both arms and held her away from him. His eyes posed a silent question to hers before lowering to her abdomen. "Are you?"

She wiggled out of his grasp. "Certainly not!" She hoped.

"Well, then, see? Things can go on just as they have before," he said happily.

His cavalier attitude was intended to boost her spirits and alleviate her anxiety. Instead, it annoyed her. Having restored her self-image with a few sweet words, and soothed her guilty conscience with a plausible rationalization for her behavior, he had dismissed the whole episode, secure in the knowledge that he still had her friendship. Unscathed, he had hurdled what had grown into a major stumbling block in her mind.

Damned if she'd let him know it, though!

"Oh, Worth, I'm so relieved that you feel like that," she said, giving him a dazzling smile. "Now I feel free to share my good news with you."

"Good news?"

"Josh—the handsome, rich gynecologist I told you about, remember?—didn't give up on me. He came by this afternoon and invited me out to dinner tomorrow night."

Worth's smile took on the consistency of setting cement. "How nice. He doesn't take no for an answer, does he?"

"Thankfully not," she said, laying a coquettish hand against the base of her throat and laughing breathlessly.

"My love life's improving too. I've decided to forgive Greta."

Cyn's laughter sputtered and died. "Greta's the one who—"

"Stood me up last weekend. She's been begging my forgiveness ever since."

"Oh."

"The best thing about having a tiff," he said expansively, "is making up."

"Yes, isn't it?" She raised her arm and pointedly consulted her wristwatch, even as she envisioned him up to his neck in a cauldron of boiling oil.

"Lord, look how late it is! I guess I'll have to trust Charlie to get Mother safely home."

She covered a huge fake yawn. "I can't wait up for her. I'm exhausted and need to get some rest."

Turning, he headed for the front door, muttering as he went. "You don't have to ask me twice."

"What was that, Worth? I didn't quite catch it."

"I said that I've got a big day tomorrow too, and should be home in bed."

"Are you angry? You sound angry." He was moving so swiftly, it was difficult for her to keep up. She collided with him when he reached the front door and came to an abrupt halt.

"No, I'm not angry. Why should I be angry?"

"No reason I can think of."

"I'm in a hurry to get home, that's all. Thank you for reminding me how late it is. I need to call Greta and firm up our plans for tomorrow night." He leaned in closer and whispered, "Not that it really matters what we do first."

She couldn't miss his meaning and wondered why she wasn't able to tease or make a joke out of his sexual dalliances the way she had only a week ago.

"Well, have fun," she said breezily.

"Oh, I intend to." He snapped his fingers. "Which reminds me, I need to stop by the drugstore on my way home. Just because I slipped up last Saturday night doesn't mean that I'm not sexually responsible. When you have as many women as I do . . . well, you know what I mean. A guy can't be too careful."

He wouldn't be nearly so handsome, she thought, if she ripped out every hair on his head by the root. "I'm glad you stopped by tonight, Worth, so we could clear the air about that other matter."

"What other matter? Oh, you mean what happened in Mexico? Hell, I've already forgotten it," he said with an indifferent shrug.

"Well, so have I!"

"I'm standing right here, Cyn. You don't have to shout."

"It's just that I'm so glad we're still friends."

"Friends. You bet. To the bitter end. It would take more than a roll in the hay to come between good friends like us."

She bared her teeth in a facsimile of a smile. "How sweetly put."

"Well, you're the one who called it a one-night stand."

"Which is all it was, wasn't it?"

"Damn right. Good night."

"Good night."

"Oops, almost forgot." Reaching into the pocket of his windbreaker, he gathered up about ten thousand scraps of paper and threw them into the air. They fell around them like snow.

"What's that?" Cyn cried.

"The check you mailed me for your share of the expenses."

"I want to pay for my half."

His grin was sickeningly smug. "You did."

She slammed the door, almost smashing his nose and the toes of his run-down Docksides.

Fuming, she marched toward her bedroom. She tried to think of one good reason why she shouldn't submit to a self-indulgent crying jag.

Her son was happy and well-adjusted, but he didn't have a daddy and that deficiency would probably affect him in later life. Her mother was getting married and she was glad about it, but when Ladonia moved to Charlie's, it would leave a huge vacancy in this house. Tomorrow was Friday, the end of a ghastly week, but that only meant she was one day away from enduring her dinner date with Dr. Josh Masters.

She burst into tears.

Ten

Ladonia's sparkling light brown eyes were especially bright as she waited in her bedroom for her second wedding ceremony to begin.

"You look beautiful, Mother." Cyn was able to say it with honesty and pride. "The dress is perfect. Straight out of an F. Scott Fitzgerald novel."

The golden beige georgette was beaded across the shoulders of the blouson bodice. Its flared skirt swirled from a snug-fitting hip band. It would have been a disaster on anyone else, but Ladonia was slim enough to carry it off.

"Thank you, Cynthia. You look lovely too."

Her dress was a deeper shade of gold than her mother's, but just as romantic and feminine, a departure from the tailored suits she wore to the hospital every day.

They heard the taped music begin playing in the living room.

"Oh, dear," Ladonia said, taking a deep breath.

"Nervous?"

"Some. Yes. Do you really think these earrings are okay?"

"They're perfect." Cyn still had her eye on the diamond drops her mother was unsure of as she crossed to answer the soft tap on the door. Expecting the minister, she fell back a step when she found herself face-to-face with Worth, looking spectacular in a dark three-piece suit and baby blue shirt.

"What are you doing here?"

"I came for the bride." His eyes moved beyond her to Ladonia. He gave a soft whistle. "I really blew it this time, letting you get away."

He stepped past Cyn, who still hadn't recovered from the shock of seeing him after two weeks without hearing a word. In times past, they'd called one another at least once a week even if they didn't have anything significant to say.

"These are from your groom, who, I must say from a purely objective point of view, looks extremely handsome, if a bit weak-kneed."

He extended Ladonia a beautiful bouquet of gold roses, white orchids, and baby's breath. "He's an adorable man," she said. Her eyes got misty as she lovingly gazed at the bouquet.

"He's a lucky devil." Worth gave her a swift hug. "Ready, love?"

Taking his arm, she slid her hand into the crook of his elbow. Turning, they confronted Cyn.

"We'd better not keep them waiting any longer, Cynthia, or Charlie might think I've chickened out."

"What's Worth doing here?"

"He's escorting me to my groom." Ladonia patted his arm affectionately and smiled up at him.

"Why?"

"I asked him to," she said. "He graciously consented and I couldn't be happier if I had a son to escort me. Now, I really don't think we should delay our appearance any longer or the guests will get restless."

Cyn turned suddenly and stalked down the hallway, a little too militantly for her pace to be classified a bona fide wedding march. She paused at the entrance of the living room until she felt Ladonia and Worth move into place behind her; then she matched her footsteps to the music and glided toward where the minister and Charlie were standing in front of the fireplace.

She'd taken special pains with the decorations and was pleased to note that the room looked beautifully romantic with the afternoon sunlight filtering through the blinds. Bowls of roses were scattered throughout. A crystal vase of calla lilies graced the glass coffee table. The mantel was decorated with greenery, more roses, and flickering vanilla-scented votive candles.

Charlie's two sons, their wives, and assorted grandchildren were seated on the sofas and chairs. One of the older girls had been placed in charge of Brandon. Cyn gave Josh Masters a faltering smile as she moved past him. Ladonia had urged her to invite him to the wedding to "balance things out."

As she turned and faced the minister, Cyn caught sight of an unfamiliar woman perched on the arm of a sofa. Earlier, she'd been introduced to all of Charlie's family; and couldn't imagine who this late arrival was, until she saw her wink at Worth as he escorted Ladonia toward her groom.

Not only had he shown up at what should have been a private family affair, he'd had the gall to bring a date!

She shot him a fulminating glare as he removed Ladonia's hand from his arm, kissed it, then extended it to Charlie. Having performed his part of the ceremony, he joined his date.

The minister began by reading a scripture, but the sweetness of the ceremony had been spoiled for Cyn. She tried concentrating on the radiant, loving smiles Ladonia and Charlie exchanged, but found her eyes roving toward the couple at the end of the sofa. Once, when Worth caught her looking at him, she whipped her gaze back toward the wedding couple.

Brandon became restless about midway through the ceremony. Cyn was aware of his fidgeting, which Charlie's granddaughter was having a tough time putting a stop to.

At a signal from Worth, Brandon went to stand beside him. Worth laid his hand on the boy's head, which Brandon inclined to rest against Worth's thigh.

Her mother and her son adored the rat.

"With the authority vested in me by God and the laws of this state, I now pronounce you man and wife. Charlie, you may kiss your bride."

There was a round of applause. Hugs and hearty congratulations were passed around the room. Cyn ended up in Josh's embrace. He aimed a kiss toward her lips, but caught her cheek when she quickly turned her head aside. "Come and meet Charlie."

"Dr. Masters, it's such a pleasure to meet you finally." Charlie's guileless features were wreathed in happiness as the two shook hands.

"Likewise. Having met your bride, it's no mystery to me where Cyn gets her beauty." Turning to Ladonia, he sandwiched her hand between his. "Much happiness, Mrs. Tanton."

He was very handsome. His manners were flawless. He was considered extremely desirable.

Cyn couldn't bear to be near him.

"Josh, excuse me a minute. I need to check with the caterer."

After making certain that Brandon was being supervised by two of his new step-cousins, she headed for the kitchen to signal the caterer that everyone would soon be migrating into the dining room for the cold buffet.

As she was giving finishing touches to the dining table, Worth approached with his date, who was decorating his right side.

"Cyn, this is Greta. Greta, Cyn."

"I'm so pleased to meet you, Cyn."

"Nice to meet you too."

Greta was tall, blond, beautiful, and buxom. She looked like a Swedish fitness-poster girl. Adding insult to injury, she seemed intelligent and genuinely nice. Cyn hated her on sight.

"I was glad you could go to Mexico with Worth a few weeks ago," Greta said. "It would have been a shame to waste the tickets."

"He told you?" She slid a chilly glance at Worth, who was pilfering olives from a relish tray. He popped one into his mouth, giving her an ingenuous smile as he vigorously chewed.

"He said he'd taken his oldest and dearest friend."

"He's a real doll." "Oldest and dearest" made her sound like a maiden aunt, no doubt intentionally.

"There you are." Josh's voice barely preceded his hands, which slid possessively around her hips as he moved to stand behind her. "I haven't seen near enough of you today."

"I'm sorry, Josh. I've got duties to attend to." Cyn noticed that Worth was no longer chewing, and his angelic eyes had narrowed to dangerous slits as he stared down at Josh's hands, which were still resting on her hips. "Josh, I'd like for you to meet one of my late husband's friends, Worth Lansing, and his date, Greta."

The men squared off to assess each other as they shook hands.

"Dr. Masters? I read an article about you in *D Magazine,* didn't I?" Greta inquired pleasantly when it became apparent that neither man was going to acknowledge the introduction beyond the obligatory handshake.

Josh turned his attention to her. Cyn used the opportunity to slip away with a murmured apology for having to see to the other wedding guests. Worth was left glowering.

Glasses of champagne were raised to the bride and groom in toasts. Finger food was consumed. Wedding cake was sliced and served. Photographs were taken. The mood was merry.

Cyn was miserable.

She divided her time between acting as hostess, and trying to avoid Josh's groping hands, and ignoring the attention Worth lavished on Greta.

When she didn't think she could take any more, she sidled up to her mother, who was chatting with one of Charlie's daughters-in-law. "Mother, all your things are laid out and ready to pack, aren't they?"

"Yes, dear, why?"

"Why don't you visit with your guests as long as possible. I'll go pack everything for you."

"How sweet of you to offer, Cyn. I'm enjoying this so much. Isn't Charlie's family wonderful? They've accepted me without a qualm."

"I'm delighted, but not the least surprised. Why wouldn't they welcome you into their family? You're the best. I love you, Mother."

They embraced and kissed each other's cheeks. Cyn realized just how much she was going to miss having her mother under the same roof. Both were misty-eyed when the hug finally ended.

"By the time you come in to change, I'll have your suitcases ready to load into the car."

"Thank you, dear."

Managing to slip out unseen by Josh, who had the tracking instincts of a panther, Cyn left the party and went into her mother's bedroom.

Ladonia was well organized. Everything she was taking on her honeymoon, a two-week trip to Hawaii, had already been folded and laid out on the bed. Cyn had packed one suitcase and was working on the second when Worth came in after rapping sharply on the door.

"If you're looking for the little boys' room—"

"Ladonia thought you might need some help." He closed the door behind him.

"Doing what? Folding lingerie?" She gave

him an icy once-over. "Come to think of it, you'd probably be an expert at that."

"Not at all," he retorted with a smirk. "My expertise lies in removing it."

She snatched a swimsuit off the bed, rolled it into a ball, and stuffed it into the suitcase. "I can handle this, but thanks for the offer. You'd better get back to Gretel before she gets lost."

"It's *Greta,*" he corrected, "and what's that crack supposed to mean?"

"That she's so dumb she probably couldn't find her rear with both hands."

"She doesn't need to."

"Oh, I get it. You'd find it for her."

"With both hands."

"It's big enough," she muttered as she crammed a pair of beach sandals into the bag. "Matches the rest of her. Just how tall is she, anyhow?"

He pushed back his suit coat and shoved both hands into his pants pockets. From his rigid stance and fierce facial expression, Cyn judged he needed to restrain his hands or he might start punching the walls. His vest fitted his narrow waist to a tee. He looked gorgeous. Damn him.

"So that's the famous Dr. Masters," he said.

"That's him."

"Are you two an item?"

"If you wanted to know, you could have called and asked."

"You haven't called me either."

"The last couple of weeks have been hectic—planning the wedding, shopping with Mother for her trousseau."

"*She* found time to call me."

"Well, obviously she had something to say to you."

"And you don't?"

She slammed the lid over the suitcase and snapped it shut. "Now that you mention it, yes."

"Well?"

"I think it's really pathetic to see an adult male salivating over a girl just because she's well-built. As your friend, I feel it's my duty to tell you how ridiculous you look fawning over her."

He moved closer, bearing down on her. "As long as we're being so *friendly*," he said in a growling tone, "I feel it's my duty as Tim's friend to warn you about slick hustlers like Dr. Masters."

"I'm a big girl. I can take care of myself."

"I'll bet that on the first date, Masters took you to a very romantic restaurant."

"The Old Warsaw."

"Perfect! Right down to the strolling violins. The second date would have been to someplace trendy, chic, and fun."

"Sfoozi's."

"Mm-hmm. A place to see and be seen so he could impress you with what a man-about-town he is and how lucky you are to be with him."

Feigning boredom, she glanced beyond his shoulder into a wall mirror and fiddled with her hair. "Is all this going somewhere, Worth?"

"You bet it is. The next time he asks you out, it will be to his place, or somewhere equally intimate. He'll suggest a cozy evening for two." He poked her chest with his index finger. "That's when he'll make his move, when you're relaxed and mellowed by fine wine and soft music. And if he gets you into his hot tub, you're as good as made."

"Speaking from experience?"

"Years of it."

"Well, I'm not one of your bimbos."

"That's my point, Cyn. You're new to the game. A babe in the woods. The rules have changed since you dated Tim back in college. You're my friend, and I'm afraid you'll get hurt."

"You think I'm stupid and unsophisticated."

"Naive."

"Thanks for the words of caution, Worth, but I know the rules of the game better than you think."

Before she could turn away, he caught her shoulders. "Does my advice come too late?"

With cool defiance she asked, "Aren't you the one who said, 'So, if you like him, let him have you'?"

He slowly nodded his head as though he'd just reached a conclusion. "Well, that's not surprising, I guess."

Her eyes sharpened to green points. "Why do you say that?"

Bending down, he whispered tauntingly, "Because I know just how little effort it takes to make you wet."

Her palm cracked against his cheek.

Ladonia chose that moment, while the reverberation of the slap was still palpable, to sail through the door. She drew up short. "What in the world was that?"

Slowly Worth backed away from Cyn, though their eyes were still locked in murderous combat. "Cyn doesn't need any help. She's doing fine on her own." Having said that, he brushed past Ladonia and stamped out.

Studying her daughter's pallid face, Ladonia closed the door. "All right, Cynthia. This has gone on long enough. What has happened between you and Worth?"

From somewhere deep within herself, Cyn garnered enough bravado to face her mother. "Nothing," she replied innocently. "What could have happened?"

"I asked first."

She foundered for something plausible to say. "I didn't think it was in very good taste for him to bring a date today. I can't imagine why he did."

"Probably because I suggested it."

"Oh, well, in that case, I guess it was okay." With an awkward wave of her hand, which still stung from slapping him, she indicated the packed suitcases. "Let me help you change, Mother, then you and Charlie can be on your way." Forcing a brittle smile, she said with jarringly false levity, "Mustn't keep the anxious bridegroom waiting."

The house was finally empty, save for Brandon, who was asleep in his room, and Cyn, who was sitting in the den staring moodily into the fireplace and using up what was left of the vanilla-scented candles. She'd transferred them from the living-room mantel so she could enjoy them.

Shortly after Charlie and Ladonia had raced to his car parked at the curb, being pelted by rice and good wishes, the guests had departed. Josh had been the last to go, and only then because Cyn had insisted.

"Why don't you get out for a while?" he had suggested. "You've been on your feet all day. Let me cook something at my place. We can call a sitter for Brandon."

Worth's prediction echoed as noisily as Quasimodo's bells in her ears. "Thanks anyway, Josh, but I need to straighten up the house."

"I'll help. When we're finished I'll send out for Chinese. We'll spend a quiet evening together."

She shook her head. "Really, I'm exhausted and not the least bit hungry."

Grudgingly he'd finally said good-bye, claimed a kiss, and left.

Even after the caterer had cleared out, there was still a lot to do to put the house right again. Brandon was acting ornery and insisted he was hungry even though she knew better. She finally opened a can of pasta and meat sauce, which was a gastronomical, not to mention nutritional, atrocity. He played in it until she whisked it away and trundled him off to bed.

Now, dressed in comfy sweats and oversize socks, she sat staring into the fireplace, enjoying the absence of any noise except for the crackling of the burning logs.

When the doorbell rang, she groaned. "I can't believe it." Deciding to wait it out and hope whoever it was would go away, she hunkered deeper into the sofa and hugged a cushion to her chest. After the third peal of the chime, afraid that the racket would wake up Brandon, she tossed the cushion aside and rolled to her feet.

It was Worth.

"Wha'cha doing?"

"Thinking seriously about slamming the door in your face."

"Hey, I'm the one who got slapped to-day." He worked his jaw with comic exaggeration and rubbed it gently, wincing as he did.

Cyn ducked her head in chagrin. "I've never struck anyone in my life."

"Then I guess I should feel honored."

"I'm sorry, Worth."

"You were sorely provoked. I don't recall ever saying anything quite that nasty to a woman before." Their gazes held for a moment. "May I come in? Do I smell wood burning in the fireplace?" He sensed her hesitancy and asked, "You're not, uh, entertaining, are you?"

"Like this?" She spread her arms to indicate her sloppy attire. He mimicked her gesture, drawing her attention to the fact that he was similarly dressed. She stepped aside and nodded him into the hallway. "I can't promise I'll be good company. I'm very tired."

"One glass of champagne and then I'll split."

"Champagne?" she asked over her shoulder as she led him through the dark house toward the firelight glow that pervaded the den.

"Surely you've got a bottle left over."

"Several, in fact."

"We'll start with one. You get it and the glasses while I'm putting another log on the fire."

"We've got dozens of finger sandwiches left too. Canapés, mints, nuts?"

"Just champagne," he called as she headed for the kitchen.

When she returned with two fluted crystal glasses and a bottle of champagne, flames were licking the new logs. "Where's Brandon?" he asked as he deftly worked the cork from the bottle.

She held out the glasses. "In bed and fast asleep, thank heaven. All the attention he got today went straight to his head. He was being a monster." She raised her brimming glass. "What are we drinking to?"

"Friendship."

Cyn cocked her head, her expression wary.

"Friendship?" He repeated the word but put a different inflection on it.

"I only slap my very best friends," she said, clinking her glass against his.

Chuckling companionably, they settled down on the sofa facing the fire and placed their feet on the large square coffee table in front of them. They slouched in the soft cushions, resting their heads on the back of the sofa.

"I behaved like a total jerk this afternoon," he said.

"I was being a bitch." She rolled her head to one side so she could look at him. "I don't know why."

He moved his head to bring them face-to-face. "Don't you?"

"No."

"You were jealous, Cyn."

"Jealous? Of the blond bombshell, who wasn't at all dumb as I said, but very intelligent and articulate? Jealous of a skein of moonbeam-blond hair and big blue eyes, among other big attributes? Don't be ridiculous." Depositing her champagne glass on the table, she stood up, moved to the fireplace, and picked up the poker.

"You're not going to clobber me with that, are you?"

She had the grace to laugh at her own expense. "Actually I was going to stir the coals, but now that you mention it . . ."

She raised the poker threateningly over her head and snarled before dropping it back onto the hearth. "Okay, I confess. I couldn't stand watching you with her."

"What's wrong with Greta?"

"Nothing. Not a single thing," she said ruefully. She returned to the sofa and flopped down beside him again. "I thought you'd be tucked into bed with her by now."

He shrugged as he reached for a strand of Cyn's hair. "Lack of initiative. What about Dr. Open-and-say-ahh?"

She yanked her head back, freeing her hair from the fingers that were absently playing with it. "Was that intentionally crude?"

"Absolutely."

Her censorious expression lasted but a few seconds. "I sent him home."

"Did he ask to stay?"

"Yes, after I declined going to his place and letting him cook dinner for me." She held up both hands in a gesture of surrender. "I know, I know. You don't have to say, 'I told you so.' He couldn't have been any more predictable if you'd handed him a script."

To Worth's credit, he let the subject drop without gloating. "What smells so good?"

"The candles."

"Oh. I thought it might be new bath powder."

"No."

"Not that yours needed improvement. I can't step out of the shower anymore without missing the smell of it lingering in the bathroom."

Their eyes met, and the sudden impact momentarily knocked the wind out of them. Staring at him made her body feel warm and fluid, heavy but weightless. After a long moment she looked away. He was all too appealing with his hair falling over his brow. The fairer strands picked up every ray of light dancing out of the fire.

"I guess the honeymooners are in L.A. by now," she remarked inanely.

"Guess so."

"They're spending the night at the Bonaventure and flying to Hawaii tomorrow."

"It'll be a nice trip for them."

"Mother's always wanted to go to Hawaii."

"Charlie seems perfect for her."

"Perfect."

"Not that he's done too shabbily for himself."

"I thought Mother looked gorgeous today."

"A real knockout. The ceremony was nice."

"Very sweet and romantic."

"The preacher said all the right things."

"I thought so."

"Cyn?"

"Hmm?"

"Screw being buddies."

Eleven

He pulled her into his embrace. She went willingly. Their mouths fastened together. They sank into the sofa cushions until they were prone, his body partially covering hers.

"Cyn, dammit," he grated when he came up for air. "Tell me you haven't let that grinning quack touch you with so much as his stethoscope."

Twining her fingers through his hair, she pulled his head down for another hot kiss, eliminating the need for any vocal response. When the scorching kiss ended and he burrowed his face in her neck, she asked, "What about Greta?"

"Haven't touched her. I told her I was experiencing temporary impotence."

Cyn pushed him up and stared at him with wide-eyed incredulity. He readjusted their bodies and nudged her middle. "I was lying, of course."

Her green eyes glazed with renewed passion as she reached for him again. Small breathy sounds of mounting desire and insufficient gratification joined those of the happily popping blaze in the fireplace.

She was hot—from the fleece-lined sweatsuit, and the warm room, and Worth's stroking hands. They eventually made their way to her waist and slipped beneath the sweatshirt.

"Cyn, what I said this afternoon . . ."

"Yes?"

"It was unforgivable."

"Yes."

"But that's what I was thinking about." His hands found her breasts soft and full and feverish. He gently manipulated their rising crests. "I can't get it out of my mind. God knows I've tried. But I can't forget how wet you were the first time I touched you."

She groaned softly and shifted restlessly beneath him, angling her hips upward.

"You're so small," he said raspily. "It felt so damn good to be inside you."

He pushed up her top and kissed her between the ribs just beneath her sternum. His mouth moved to her breast, kissed the responsive tip, then the full curve, which yielded when he nuzzled it.

"Worth." She sighed, arching her throat.

As his hands bracketed her rib cage, his mouth slowly worked its way down the center of her body, testing, teasing, tasting. His lips gently sucked at her skin. His tongue left damp patches on it. He took a love bite, lightly scratching the surface with his teeth.

The caresses were entrancing. Through drowsy eyes she studied the flickering patterns of light and shadow on the ceiling. She deeply inhaled the heady scent of the candles, which was almost as drugging as the effects of the champagne that fizzed inside her head.

The words of the wedding ceremony drifted through the chambers of her mind. Pretty words like "cherish." Romantic phrases like "keeping her only unto thyself."

Suddenly her vision cleared and, with it, her thinking.

"Worth, we can't." She pushed him away and scrambled off the sofa. He struggled to regain his balance and blink her into focus.

"What's the matter?"

"We can't."

"I planned ahead this time. I've got something in my car."

"It's not that."

"Then what?" He gulped in several drafts of oxygen. "I'm in pain here, Cyn."

Miserably she wrung her hands. "I know the feeling, but . . . but we still can't be casual lovers."

"We can't be pals either," he said testily. "We proved that today. When I saw Masters' hands on you, I thought seriously about ripping out his throat."

"I was deliberately rude to Greta."

"So we've both been naughty. Let's promise to do better next time. But right now I'd like to get on with what we had going here."

"Don't you see?" she cried, raising her fists to her temples. "Tonight we're falling for the same scam as before. If we surrender to it, we'll be worse off afterward than we are now."

"Impossible," he groaned as he eased himself to his feet. "I'm going to need more champagne." He hobbled toward the door. Over his shoulder he added, "A whole lot more."

When he returned, Cyn was relieved to see that his posture had improved, but he was swigging champagne straight from a fresh bottle. "What scam?"

"The romantic atmosphere," she said from where she was now seated on the stone ledge of the hearth. "Weddings are sentimental, romantic affairs that make everybody feel a little marshmallowy inside."

"I never really thought about it."

"Weddings combine the spiritual with the physical, romance with religion. They make everybody in attendance, no matter how callous the individual might be, believe in true and everlasting love."

He drank from his bottle and wiped his lips with the back of his hand. "You're right. My eyes got damp today when Charlie and Ladonia exchanged vows. I remember other weddings too. Lord knows I've attended

scores of them. My dates afterward were always particularly—" He broke off and
glanced at her. "Not that I'm implying you're
just another post-wedding date."

"Thank you." She bowed her head over
her restless hands. "Weddings put everybody in a romantic frame of mind. Combine
that with the champagne, the candles, the
solitude, the fireplace tonight, and you've
got . . ." She made a small motion with her
shoulders. "It's as evocative as the tropical
ambience of Acapulco. We fell victim to it."

"Hmm, maybe." The champagne sloshed
in the bottle as he raised it to his mouth
again.

"Maybe?"

"Come here, Cyn," he said, smiling. "I'm
not going to bite."

"You were." Even as she reminded him,
she got up and resumed her place beside
him on the couch.

With his other four digits curled around
the neck of the champagne bottle, he raised
that hand and touched the corner of her
mouth with his index finger. His other hand
took hers and pressed it against his lap. His
improved posture had been deceptive.

"It took more than a few sweet-smelling

candles and a fireplace to get me like this, Cyn."

A geyser of heat shot upward from her thighs and spread across her breasts. Hastily she withdrew her hand, left the sofa again, and moved toward the mantel, where she needlessly rearranged the framed photographs of Brandon. "You said you wouldn't—"

"Bite. That's all I said I wouldn't do. Cyn." He refused to say more until she turned to face him, which she did reluctantly. "We have a built-in desire for each other."

"For each other or for sex?"

"I could have had sex with Greta. You could have had Masters."

"I didn't want—"

"Exactly! And I didn't want Greta. I wanted you."

Caught in a trap of her own making, Cyn backed down. She lowered herself to the stone hearth again. "I guess there's no point in denying that we're sexually attracted, is there?"

"It would be stupid. Neither of us is stupid. That's why I came over here tonight. I thought we should approach this dilemma like adults and not a couple of jealous adolescents."

He set the second bottle of champagne on the coffee table beside the first one and looked down at his hands. "However, if when I got here I'd found you locked in a carnal embrace with the gynecologist, all my good intentions of behaving like a rational grown-up would have been shot to hell."

"It was pure torture to imagine you with Greta." Lifting anguished eyes to his, she asked, "What are we going to do, Worth? We can't go on like this."

"You can say that again," he grumbled.

After a lengthy silence, Cyn voiced the most obvious, but also most dismal, option. "We could stop seeing each other altogether for a while."

"The last two weeks nearly drove me crazy."

"Me too," she admitted. "Besides, it would hurt Brandon. You're the only hands-on contact he has with a man. I'd have to make up something to tell Mother. She already senses that Mexico altered our relationship."

"Smart woman, Ladonia." His fingers did

pushups against each other as he contemplated their problem. "Making love did alter our relationship, Cyn. It'll never be the same. We can't be just friends any longer. We've proved that."

Mournfully she sighed. "So we *will* have to stop seeing each other."

"No," he said slowly, "we'll have to do it again."

Her expression went completely blank for several seconds before her eyes narrowed and glinted with anger. "Have an affair? One you can walk away from whenever you feel like it? No way, Mr. Lansing."

"Will you please hear me out before flying off the handle?"

He bounded off the couch and took the necessary steps to bring him toe to toe with her. He towered over her where she still sat on the hearth. So she wouldn't feel at such a disadvantage, she came to her feet.

"I honestly don't know what'll develop," he said, "but we owe it to ourselves to sleep together at least once more, Cyn. We can't resolve this thing until we do."

She rolled her eyes. "I can't wait to hear this rationalization."

"You said that tonight and Mexico were

just flukes, that we were victims of setting and circumstance."

Mistrustfully she nodded, wondering where he was taking this argument.

"Okay, we need to find out if that's all they were."

"They were."

"Then you've got nothing to worry about and there's no harm in trying it." It was a standoff. They all but pawed the ground. "Listen," he said, impatiently raking back his hair, "admit that the sex was terrific."

Her eyes lowered to his throat. She gave a terse nod.

"Okay. And admit that we don't have to harbor any guilt over Tim because nothing but friendship sparked between us until Acapulco. Agreed?"

"Agreed."

Subconsciously she rubbed the third finger of her left hand, where she knew there was still a ring of pale skin. She had removed her wedding band upon her return from Mexico, feeling she had betrayed Tim, although she knew that Worth's reasoning was valid.

"Good. You've conceded points one and two." He collected his thoughts. "For clarity,

I'll combine points three and four. If only the mood was responsible, we'll find out soon enough, and until we do find out, neither one of us is going to be worth a damn. We can't be functional professionals while trapped within this turbulent emotional climate."

She frowned at his elaborate phraseology. "That sounded rehearsed."

"It was. For about six days."

"Six days? If you've been thinking about this that long, why did you bring a date to the wedding?"

"Spite. Which brings up another crucial point. We've never played games with each other, Cyn. I hate playing games with you."

"Same here. Any other time, I would have been batting off Josh's hands. I let him paw me today because I knew it was getting to you. And everything you've said has merit, no matter how loftily you phrased it. I've only been going through the motions at work. I've been cranky. I can't keep my mind on anything. It was a superhuman feat to plan the wedding."

"So what do you say?"

She fidgeted nervously, shifting her weight from one stockinged foot to the other. His sexy dishevelment might influence her decision, so she tried not to take his looks into account, but base her decision strictly on the pragmatic arguments he'd set forth.

"It would be sort of like a scientific experiment, wouldn't it?"

"Exactly. We'll try it and see how it goes. If it's no good, we'll know that the time in Mexico was an accident and resume being just good friends."

"And if it is, uh, good?"

"We'll cross that bridge when we come to it." He pressed her for an answer.

"Well," she said, stretching out the word as she gnawed her inner cheek, "I guess we could."

"Ah, Cyn, that's great."

Smiling, he reached out to draw her into his arms. She laid restraining hands against his chest. "But not tonight."

His smile collapsed. His arms dropped lifelessly to his sides. "Oh. Sure. Right. Of course. How come?"

"We're still too caught up in post-wedding emotionalism."

Swearing beneath his breath, he glanced at the flickering candles, the champagne bottles, the crackling fire, and Cyn's kiss-swollen lips. "I guess you're right," he said with a grudging sigh. "So when? Tomorrow?"

After several rounds of give-and-take, they settled on the following weekend. Worth wasn't pleased. "That's seven days," he complained.

"Which should give us plenty of time to clear our heads and approach this pragmatically. Otherwise, it wouldn't prove a thing and we might just as well not go through with it."

Afraid that she would back out, he consented, but insisted on kissing her good night before he left. She gladly accepted the sleek exploration of his tongue inside her mouth while he held her body firmly against his, but when his hands moved to her breasts, she eased him away.

"Not yet," she managed to say in spite of her shortness of breath.

She spent all day Sunday with Brandon, since he would have to go to a day-care center while Ladonia was away. He didn't mind. He loved playing with the other children.

Her work calendar was filled with appointments, which ordinarily made the days fly. Instead they seemed to crawl at a snail's pace toward Friday.

On Wednesday she let Brandon invite Shane Lattimore to sleep over in exchange for his staying at Shane's house on the coming Friday night.

She blushed when she asked Mrs. Lattimore if they could swap favors. Lying, she said that her need to be away overnight was work-related. Thankfully, over the telephone Mrs. Lattimore could see neither her red cheeks nor the guilt in her eyes.

To Worth's annoyance, she had insisted that they not see each other until their first official "date." Not to be put off, he called her every night and sometimes during the day.

"Where'll we do it?"

Due to a particularly heavy caseload that day, she was having lunch at her desk. Cradling the telephone between her chin and shoulder as she peeled a banana, she quipped, "In a bed, I would imagine."

"Very funny. Which bed?"

"A hotel? I'll pay half."

"Nix. Unless you want another torn-up check on your floor. How about my place? We'll have dinner here too."

"I don't know, Worth," she hedged.

"I've already planned the menu. Besides, my apartment is the most logical place."

"The pleasure palace."

"It does have its creature comforts."

She thought about the thick sheepskin rug on the living-room floor and the hot tub in the black marble master bath. "I guess so." Her reluctance stemmed from a mix of trepidation and excitement.

"Great. I'll pick you up at—"

"No, I'll drive myself over."

"So you'll have a means of escape."

"My microwave soup is getting cold."

"Coward!" he shouted into the receiver as she hung up. She barely had time to finish her desktop lunch before the secretary announced her one-o'clock appointment. It was Sheryl Davenport.

"Come in." Cyn rose to greet her. "How did you get out of class?"

"I told them I had a dental appointment."

"Sit down. How are you feeling?" Cyn returned to her chair behind the desk.

"I've been getting sick every morning."

"You look like you've lost a few pounds." Cyn noticed the dark circles under her eyes too. Medication could relieve morning sickness, but that was the least of Sheryl's complications. "How are you doing otherwise?"

"Not very well. Daddy's pressuring me to enroll in this course that prepares you to take the SAT." She raised her hands, then let them fall uselessly back into her lap. "He's thinking college-entrance exams and I'm thinking alternatives to pregnancy."

"Then you haven't told your parents yet?"

"No. I'd be dead if I had."

"Don't say that, Sheryl. It isn't true."

"As good as dead," she said miserably. "Mrs. McCall, I don't know what I'm going to do."

"Did you read the literature I gave you?"

"Yes."

"But you're no closer to a decision?"

She shook her head. "I think I want to put the baby up for adoption—you know, the kind where I'd get to see it periodically."

"Open adoption."

"Yes. I'd like for my baby to know me, to know that I loved him and didn't just give him away because I didn't want him. But whenever I envision telling my parents, I . . . I just don't think I can." She choked up and began to cry.

For the rest of their session, Cyn tried to alleviate Sheryl's fear and desperation. It wasn't easy. By the time she left, Cyn was exhausted. The funny, wicked card she received from Worth in the afternoon mail arrived when she badly needed a boost to her spirits.

When she got to her office on Thursday morning, a dozen white roses were adorning her desk. "From Dr. Masters?" her secretary asked, hovering nearby as Cyn read the sender's card.

"No," she replied with a secretive smile. "From someone else."

"Must be nice to have so many admirers."

After the secretary returned to her duties in the outer office, Cyn read the card again. "Roses are red, Violets are blue, We used to be friends, We still are, And that's what makes it so much better."

She was laughing when Josh strolled in emanating charm and the scent of antiseptic soap. His easy smile tightened when he spotted the vase of flowers. "Roses."

"Hmm." She tucked the card into the pocket of her suit jacket.

"Birthday?"

"No special occasion."

"From anybody I should know about?"

She pondered the toes of her shoes for a moment, then raised her head. "Perhaps you should, Josh. They're from somebody very dear to me. He's—"

"He?"

"That's right. He's been very dear to me for a long time. But even if he weren't," she added, pausing to draw a breath, "it wouldn't make any difference."

"To what?"

"To us."

A lazy smile enhanced his handsome features. "I see."

"No, I don't believe you do. What I'm telling you, Josh, is that you and I have gone as far as we're going to go. There's just nothing there for me. I hope you understand."

He didn't. It was impossible for him to grasp that she preferred another man, or no man at all, to him. He created quite a scene. It wasn't losing his chance with her that rankled; it was the damage done to his ego and the time he had wasted on a pursuit that didn't pay off. She had no difficulty at all in coldly demanding that he leave her office.

After that, the rest of the day was a breeze. Before she left for home that afternoon, she snipped off one of the rosebuds and took it with her.

Half an hour later, she used her key to unlock the door of the offices of Lansing and McCall. Worth had refused to take back the key when Tim died. Since she still had an interest in the business, he wanted her to feel free to come and go at any time. This was the first time she had exercised that freedom.

As she had hoped, the office was empty. Mrs. Hardiman's typewriter was covered and the lamp on her desk turned off. Cyn passed through the anteroom and found the door to Worth's office unlocked.

Feeling like a thief, she tiptoed across the carpet to his desk and laid the rosebud on the glossy surface, along with the thank-you note she'd written on her stationery.

"Freeze!"

Squealing in fright, she spun around. He was standing in the doorway of his private lavatory, crouched in a policeman's stance, both hands extended as though they were folded around a snubnosed .38.

"You scared me half to death."

"What are you doing sneaking around my office?"

"Where's Mrs. Hardiman?"

"Gone for the day. I was just about to leave."

Their mutual smiles indicated how happy they were to see each other. He lowered his "gun" and for several moments they grinned across the space that separated them.

"I, uh, came to thank you for the roses. They were so lovely, they needed to be shared."

He moved to his desk, picked up the rose, and twirled it by the stem as he read her thank-you card aloud. " 'A poet you're not.' " He barked a short laugh, then lifted his smiling eyes to hers. "Pretty terrible, huh?"

"The worst. But I appreciated the sentiment."

Again they lapsed into another smiling and staring spell. Cyn was the first to work her way out of it. "Well, that's all I came for. If I don't leave now, I'll be late picking Brandon up."

"Wait a sec and I'll ride down in the elevator with you."

He secured his office and they left together. On the way down the hallway, they chatted about inconsequential things—the weather, their respective jobs, Brandon's week in day care—but each was aware of Worth's hand riding lightly in the small of her back.

She liked the way he carried his suit jacket over his shoulder, using one finger as a hook.

He liked the way her hair bounced against her shoulders.

His jaw was beginning to darken with a five-o'clock shadow.

Her hips swayed enticingly inside her slim skirt as she walked.

She got into the elevator and leaned into a corner of it. He occupied the opposite corner, one hand still holding his jacket and the other resting on the chrome rail that ran around the interior of the cubicle.

As they descended, their eyes remained on each other. No other passengers got on. Just before they got to the garage level, Worth dropped his jacket to the floor, reached for the red emergency button, and punched it.

The sudden stop caught Cyn off-guard. She gasped softly and grabbed hold of the rail. By the time she regained her balance, Worth had pinned her into the corner. His arms were around her waist, holding her up against him, and his mouth was feasting on hers.

The weightlessness in her tummy had nothing to do with the elevator's descent, but her own, into a fathomless well of desire so deep and dark that she didn't think she would ever find the bottom of it. Its delicious waters swirled around her, disorienting her, sucking her under.

Each kiss was more fervent than the one before it. One's greed matched the other's. Worth shoved his hands into her jacket and undid the buttons of her blouse. He parted the fabric and saw her breasts, trembling and flushed above the sheer cups of her demi-bra.

"I'm living out a fantasy," he said breathily as he ran his knuckle over the quivering flesh, then dragged it across the tight nipple beneath the straining ecru lace.

Cyn laid her hand against his hard,

scratchy cheek and drew his head down, wanting to feel his mouth against her, on her, around her. She had had fantasies too.

"I'm so hungry for a taste of you." He moaned, his lips moving against her soft cleavage.

"Do it."

"Taste you? Suck you? Lick you? What, baby? Tell me."

"All of it."

His mouth's caresses left her skin burning, her body wanting, her head ringing.

It was several seconds before they realized that an impatient tenant was demanding the use of the elevator from one of the floors above and the ringing they heard was the alarm.

Worth stepped back and awkwardly rebuttoned her blouse, mismatching the buttons with their holes. His face was suffused with the high color of passion; Cyn knew hers must look the same. She could feel the blood surging through her veins.

"Ready?" he consulted her gruffly.

She nodded and smoothed a hand over her hair, which his hands had pillaged. He put the elevator into motion again. Thankfully there was no one waiting for it in the garage. They exited and walked toward their cars.

He took her keys from her shaking hands and unlocked the driver's door. She slid beneath the wheel. He passed the keys to her through the open door, then leaned inside to brush his lips across hers.

"Tomorrow night, Cyn."

"Tomorrow night, Worth."

Twelve

"Hi."

"Hi."

"You look fantastic."

"Thank you."

Worth extended his hand and, lacing his fingers with hers, pulled her through his front door. Setting her away from him, he gave her a more thorough once-over. "Gorgeous."

She modestly lowered her eyes, though she secretly acknowledged that her primping had paid off. At the beauty salon she'd had her nails done. She'd even treated herself to a pedicure and had had her legs waxed.

Feeling slightly guilty over her self-indulgence, she had taken Brandon for pizza at his favorite restaurant, which was better known for its arcade than its food. Then she had dropped him off at his friend's house.

Her bubble bath had been long and luxuriant. She'd taken special pains with her makeup. The new dress had been another extravagance, but she had justified the outrageous price tag by reminding herself that she hadn't bought a new dinner dress in ages. The soft black jersey clung to her body. The steep V neckline was provocative, but the long double strand of faux pearls kept it respectable.

"You're almost too perfect to touch," he said. "Almost."

He moved in for a kiss. Cyn anticipated it and tilted her head to one side. Unfortunately he tilted his the same way at the same time, and instead of their lips meeting, they bumped noses. They both switched at the same time, to exactly the same angle, and banged noses again.

"You go to your right and I'll go to my right, okay?" he said, laughing softly.

"Okay."

The kiss was tender and sweet.

"Ready for frozen margaritas?" he whispered, holding his lips against hers.

"Shades of Acapulco?"

"I do my best to please."

He led her into the living room, deposited her on his white leather sofa and headed for the kitchen. He had unabashedly set the stage to seduce her. Linda Ronstadt at her most soulful was wafting from the sophisticated stereo system. Lamps formed small pools of golden light in the otherwise dim apartment. The dining table was set with china and had an exotic centerpiece comprising birds of paradise and tiger lilies.

"Damn!"

"Worth?"

"Be right there."

Curious over the delay and his evident exasperation, she left the sofa and joined him in the kitchen, where he was cursing an electronic gadget. It looked like an instrument of torture designed by a deranged dentist, or possibly a personal vibrator for the very kinky.

"What is that?" she asked, staring suspiciously at the gizmo.

"I bought it the other day. It's a handheld

blender, but I can't get the damn thing to work right." He made several unsuccessful attempts.

"Did you read the instructions?"

"Hell no. How difficult can it be?"

"Where are they?"

"I threw them away with the box."

She bit her tongue to keep from saying what a dumb thing that was to have done. As with all men not mechanically inclined, he got so frustrated he banged the blender against the countertop.

"I don't think that's going to help, Worth. Why not just use the regular blender?"

"I took it to the office when I bought this—"

"I like my margaritas icy anyway," she quickly interrupted.

"You do?"

"Yes. Really."

They ended up using spoons to eat margarita-flavored ice chips out of their glasses. Worth finally set aside his adult Popsicle and poured himself a stiff Scotch and water while continuing to disparage the high-tech blender.

"It doesn't matter, Worth."

"I just wanted everything to be perfect."

At that point they had no idea that the margarita snafu would be the high point of the evening.

Worth's cutlery clattered onto his plate as he shoved it away. "I paid forty dollars for these steaks. Not that I mind the expense. I just expected them to be edible!"

"Are you sure he said all you had to do was warm them up?"

He'd told her earlier that he'd bought them from one of the city's classiest restaurants. Cyn swallowed the bite she'd been chewing for so long her jaws were aching. The meat was still the consistency of shoe leather and not nearly as tasty.

"I got instructions from the chef himself. He promised they'd be *magnifique*." He kissed his fingertips, mimicking the French chef who had sold him not only the steaks but also a bill of goods.

"I wasn't really hungry anyway," she lied.

She had scheduled appointments through lunch so she wouldn't have a guilty conscience about leaving early for her salon appointment. She certainly hadn't wanted any of Brandon's cardboard pizza and hadn't had time to grab a snack anywhere else.

If Worth hadn't already been exasperated

over the margaritas and the meal, she would have suggested that they raid his refrigerator and make sandwiches. It seemed more prudent, given his present state of mind, to dispense with dinner altogether.

"I'm sorry about the steaks," he said, tossing down his napkin.

"No problem. Let's just take our wine—Oh, Lord!"

Holding her wineglass aloft, she had stood and scooted her chair back. Her high heel got caught on the edge of the Oriental rug beneath the dining table. She lost her balance and dropped the glass of wine. The glass was saved. The burgundy would forever be preserved in the fibers of his pride and joy.

Cyn's knees hit the floor. "Oh, Worth, no! I can't believe I did this. Hand me a napkin. Quick."

Frantically she blotted at the ruby stain. "What's good for wine?"

"Cheese," he said dismally.

"I mean to get it out. Club soda? Vinegar? Cold water? Maybe if we dipped a towel in cold water and—"

"Forget it, Cyn." He put his hand beneath her elbow and hauled her to her feet. "I'm sure somebody can get it out. An expert dry cleaner. Probably. Maybe."

"Worth, I could just die," she wailed. He had dumped a woman for leaving cellophane candy wrappers in his ashtrays. She had just ruined a pricey rug. "I remember when you bought that rug. You were so proud of it."

"Hmm. I still was. Am," he corrected quickly. "I meant 'am.' "

"Ooh." She wrung her hands in distress.

He pulled her into his arms and kissed her neck as he held her close. "Forget the damn rug, Cyn. It's not nearly as important to me as the fact that you're here and I'm about to make love to you."

She tilted her head back and gazed into his eyes as she ran her hands through his hair. "Promise?"

He kissed her deeply. "Promise."

Linking their fingers again, he led her into his bedroom. Cyn approached it timorously. She'd often teased him about how blatantly sexy it was. A zebra skin was sprawled on the floor. The bed sack was black leather, the lighting indirect, the atmosphere sybaritic. He'd already folded back the bed sack to reveal what seemed to her an acre of ivory satin sheets.

Her heart began to race. This room, she knew, had been the scene of many seductions. She wanted to be different from all the others. She wanted this night to be stamped on his memory forever.

As usually happened, she got more than she bargained for.

He turned her toward him. After whisking several light kisses across her lips, he parted them gently with his tongue, then moved it in and out of her mouth until she was gripping his shoulders and arching the front of her body into his.

"I'd like to undress you, Cyn." He whispered the request into her hair, then pulled back to read her reaction.

She wet her lips, smiled nervously, and gave a quick bob of her head. He knelt down in front of her and removed her shoes, a gesture that struck her as exceptionally sweet, but intensely sensual, as he warmly clasped her feet, one at a time, between his hands.

Standing, he placed his arms around her, reaching for the tab of her zipper. It stubbornly eluded him. He grappled with it.

"Maybe I can help," she suggested, moving his hands aside.

Or at least she tried to move them aside. His wristwatch had become snagged on the jersey. "Wait, I'm caught," he said when he sighted the problem. "Turn around."

She ducked beneath his arm and pivoted. He finally managed to wrangle his wristwatch free and undo the zipper. With the coaxing of his hands, the dress slid from her body onto the floor, but the mystique had been spoiled and the sensuality diluted.

"I don't think it did too much damage," he said, assessing the snag.

Cyn extended the mile-long thread that had been pulled out of the weave of her brand-new, very expensive dress. "No, not much."

"I'm sorry."

"It doesn't matter."

He shrugged out of his navy blazer and folded it over the arm of a chair. Cyn, striving to restore the romantic mood, assisted him in peeling the white turtleneck over his head. Bare-chested, he faced her, lifted her hand to his lips, kissed the palm, then laid it against his heart.

"You're beautiful, Cyn."

"So are you."

"I want you."

"I want you too. So much I ache."

He liked that. He grinned boyishly. "You do? Where? Here?" He folded his hand around one breast, which was temptingly encased in a sheer black lace brassiere. "Here?" He swept his thumb across her nipple. "Here?" His other hand slid warmly over her black half-slip, pressing her giving abdomen before moving lower to cup her femininity. "Here?"

His fingers moved but slightly; she drew a catchy little breath. "That makes me weak."

He scooped her into his arms and carried her to the bed. After laying her gently on the mountain of satin pillows, he left the bed only long enough to finish undressing. He was beautiful, so tawny and tanned. Naked and lean and aroused, he stretched out beside her. They came together for a hot, questing kiss that left them panting.

Coming to his knees, Worth hooked his thumbs into the waistband of her slip and removed it. Her garter belt, stockings, and bikini panties—all new, all black—robbed him of breath.

With a murmur of desire he lay down beside her again and gathered her into his arms. "Touch me, Cyn."

Shyly she placed her hand on his chest and experienced the feel of the crinkled hair against her palm and curious fingertips. He grunted with pleasure when she gave his nipple a feather-light stroke.

"Touch me . . . down there. Please."

Her hand, looking fragile against such a masculine torso, smoothed its way over his curved chest, down his flat belly, past his navel, through a wealth of body hair to the base of his manhood. Timidly she stroked the velvety length before slowly closing her fingers around it.

Worth yelped.

Cyn screamed.

The telephone rang.

Worth shot bolt upright, his face contorted in agony.

"Oh, God!" she cried, snatching back her offending hand. "What did I do? Worth? Worth! What's wrong?"

"My . . . my leg." He fell back against the pillows, rolling from side to side and thrashing his arms against the mattress.

"Your *leg*?"

"My calf. Charley horse. Cramp. Agh! Damn, that hurts."

Commiserating with him as he continued to writhe in pain, she grimaced and bit her lower lip. The telephone was on about the fourth ring. Flooded with relief to learn that she hadn't caused Worth's agonizing injury, she lifted the receiver to her ear. "Hello, uh, Lansing residence."

"Is this Mrs. McCall?"

She certainly hadn't expected anyone to call her. "Yes?"

"This is your answering service. You left this number for us to call in case of an emergency."

"That's right. What's the matter?"

"It's getting better now," Worth said through his clenched teeth as he tentatively flexed the muscle that had cramped.

"The police called and—"

"Police!" Cyn cried. "Is it Brandon? Has something happened to him? Or my mother?"

"I don't believe so. Officer Burton didn't say anything to that effect."

"Officer Burton?"

"Yes. He left a number and asked that you call it immediately."

Cyn rolled off the bed and opened the nightstand drawer in search of something to write on. "Okay, go ahead." She scrawled the number the operator gave her on the first page of Worth's little black book over the name Jennifer Adams.

"Thank you." She broke the connection and began punching out the numbers.

"Who was that? What's happened?" Worth was massaging his calf, but was looking worriedly at Cyn.

"My service. A policeman is trying to reach me."

"A policeman? What does that mean?"

"I don't know. Hello?" Her call had been answered on the first ring. "Is this Officer Burton? This is Cynthia McCall."

"Mrs. McCall," he shouted over the commotion in the background, "thank you for returning my call. I'm at the Davenport residence."

"Where? Who?"

"The Davenports' house. Out here in Bent Tree. Anyway, their daughter Sheryl is holed up in her room and refuses to come out."

Cyn combed her fingers through her hair. She was so overwhelmingly relieved to know the emergency didn't concern either Brandon or Ladonia, it hadn't immediately registered who the Davenports and their daughter Sheryl were.

"Is Sheryl all right?"

"Far as we know, but she sounds real disturbed. I found your card in her purse and thought maybe you could help."

"You say she's locked herself in her room?"

"That's right. Her parents are trying to get her to come out, or at least let one of them go in and talk to her, but she refuses." He lowered his voice. "I'm afraid she's gonna do something drastic. Get my drift?"

Anxiety settled cold and hard in Cyn's stomach. "Yes, I get your drift. What's the address and how do I get there from the Turtle Creek area?"

After scribbling down the directions over Jennifer Adams' address, she hung up and rushed across the room to retrieve her dress. Worth, sensing the urgent nature of the call, had already put on his pants and shoes and was pulling on his sweater.

"One of the girls I've been counseling is in trouble," she told him. "I've got to go to her."

"I'll drive you."

Her busy hands fell still and she looked up at him, knowing in that blinding instant that she loved him.

He hadn't asked any questions. He hadn't pressured her for an explanation. He hadn't qualified his willingness to help. He hadn't argued with her. He hadn't complained about the inconvenience imposed on him.

Just as on the day Tim had been pronounced dead at the scene of a dreadful accident, Worth was here now, offering her his unconditional support. Offering her himself.

Softly, earnestly, wishing there were time to tell him more, she simply said, "Thank you, Worth."

Thirteen

They arrived at Cyn's house well after midnight. Worth didn't ask if he should see her inside, he just did it. Cyn didn't even think to question him. It was he who unlocked the back door and flipped on light switches once they were inside.

"Are you as hungry as I am?" she asked.

"Starving. What have you got?"

"Let's see."

They put together a supper of grilled cheese sandwiches. "Better than that forty-dollar steak," he said scornfully as he bit into his second buttery, gooey sandwich.

"I'd almost forgotten the first half of this evening."

"Good. It was certainly forgettable." They glanced across the table at one another, then simultaneously started laughing. "It was a disaster!" he shouted, flinging his arms out to his sides.

"I ruined your rug," she wailed.

"I ruined your dress."

"Your rug cost a thousand times as much. But that was minimal to the damage I thought I'd done to your ... When you hollered like that, I nearly had a heart attack. I thought I had somehow emasculated you."

With a paper napkin he blotted tears of laughter from his eyes. "At the time, it didn't occur to me what you were thinking. You thought ..." He was seized by another attack of laughter that left him weak and gasping for breath.

"Poor Cyn. I should have warned you. Sometimes I get those cramps during the night, usually when I've worked out without warming up or cooling down properly. But that's the first time I've ever had a lady in bed with me when it happened."

"I could have done without that dubious honor, thank you."

When his laughter finally abated, he reached across the table for her hand. Their palms slid together; their fingers entwined.

"You were fabulous, Cyn. Really something." She gave him a quizzical look. He clarified his statement. "The way you handled the situation at the Davenports'. You have my utmost admiration and respect."

She exhaled a long, weary sigh. The laughter of a moment earlier had been a much-needed catharsis to release the tension the Davenport incident had created. Now Worth's gentle reminder of it had an immediate and sobering effect.

"I'm glad you think so, Worth, but I don't deserve any accolades. I was shaking in my shoes, afraid I'd make a bad situation even worse."

"No," he said, shaking his head, "you were terrific, once you got in there to see her."

"I have you to thank for that," she reminded him.

When they had arrived, the scene at the Davenports' mansion was even worse than Cyn had anticipated. Curious neighbors were lining the avenue, where every house demanded at least a seven-figure price.

Several police cars had heeded the security alarm, which they found out later Sheryl had tripped herself. She'd been desperate, she told Cyn, and didn't know what else to do. As she felt herself losing control, it had been a cry for help.

Mr. and Mrs. Davenport seemed more concerned about the negative attention they were attracting than they did their daughter's welfare.

When Cyn was led upstairs and introduced by Officer Burton, Mr. Davenport had demanded to know just who the hell she was and what right she had to intrude on his family's privacy.

"I called her," the policeman had said.

"Why?"

"I've been helping your daughter work out some problems, Mr. Davenport." Her voice had been calm, though she was frantic to know what was going on behind the girl's locked bedroom door.

In a stiffly authoritarian voice he had said, "If my daughter has any problems, she can come to her mother and me for help."

"Obviously not!"

"Now, see here, young woman—"

"No, *you* see, pal."

That's when Worth had taken Mr. Davenport by the arm, spun him around, and told him in straightforward syntax that Cyn was going to try to talk Sheryl into opening her door whether Davenport liked it or not.

"That's what she came for and that's what she's going to do, so get out of her way and let her do it."

Several policemen, including Officer Burton, seemed pleased that Worth had gotten tough with the real-estate mogul, whose overbearing manner had intimidated them. Officer Burton nodded at Davenport, endorsing Worth's suggestion. Puffed up like an adder, he stepped aside, allowing Cyn to approach his daughter's door.

"I didn't like the way he was talking to you," Worth said now, leaving the table and moving toward the refrigerator for a carton of milk.

"You had fire in your eyes."

"I wish now I'd punched him out."

"I'm glad you didn't, but thanks for coming to my rescue."

"Rescue, hell," he scoffed. "If anybody was rescued, it was Davenport. I thought you were about to lay into him yourself."

He refilled her glass of milk as well as his

own. "I don't expect you to discuss Sheryl's dilemma with me, Cyn, but whatever you said to her worked miracles. She seemed perfectly calm when she came out and announced to that pompous ass and Mrs. Davenport that she was ten weeks pregnant."

Cyn folded her hands around her milk glass. "When she let me in, the first thing I noticed was a bottle of sleeping pills on her nightstand. She hadn't taken any, but she told me she'd thought about swallowing all of them as an alternative to telling her parents about the baby." Her hands shook as she raised the glass of milk to her mouth.

"Then you really did prevent a disaster."

"Sheryl prevented it herself."

"But she might have gone with her instincts if you hadn't been there to put things into perspective for her."

"She said she didn't care if she lived or died. She just didn't want to destroy her child." As she recounted it for him, her eyes shimmered with tears. "I told her that was a noble and good reason not to commit suicide, but that I thought her own life was well worth saving, whether she lived up to her parents' expectations or not."

Patting his thigh, Worth reached for her hand again, pulled her out of her chair, around the table, and onto his lap. She laid her head on his shoulder and snuggled against him as his arms closed around her.

"I don't ever want to hear you say that you're ineffectual as a counselor." His voice sounded stern, but his stroking touch was light upon her hair, as was the kiss he laid on her brow. "Tonight proved otherwise. You make a vast difference in the lives of these troubled young women. As I said before, you were fabulous."

"I'm not so fabulous, Worth," she argued. "Sheryl's problems are real, life-altering. Comparatively, mine are superficial. Yet a few weeks ago I was whining about my life, wishing for a little chaos. I saw chaos for real tonight, and it wasn't pretty. No wonder my mother got so irritated with me. How selfish can one get?"

"Don't be so hard on yourself. We're all selfish when it comes to love and attention, Cyn."

"That's all Sheryl really wanted, wasn't it? Love."

Worth nodded.

"That's all I really wanted too," she murmured introspectively. That indefinable something her life had been lacking was love, a channel into which she could pour all the love she had previously reserved for her husband—erotic and romantic and wonderful love. Little had she known, however, that when she found the cure, it would hurt more than the malady.

"Well, I've got plenty of love," she said with more spirit than she felt. "From my mother. From Brandon." She sat up straight and smiled at Worth. "And I've got the very best friend anyone could wish for."

"Yeah, and don't forget you've got me too."

"You idiot." She swatted his head, but he ducked just in time. He came to his feet, lifting her with him. "Where are we going?"

"To bed. You don't look so hot."

"Thanks!"

"If your best friend won't tell you the truth, who will?"

"I am exhausted," she confessed.

"Go get your nightie on," he said when he set her down in her bedroom. "I'll turn down the bed."

She left her clothes in a heap on the bathroom floor and pulled a long T-shirt over her head. Barefoot, she padded into the bed-room.

"Climb in." He lifted the covers for her and she slid between them. He flipped a switch and the room went dark. Seconds later, the mattress sank with his weight.

"Worth?"

"Hmm?" He pulled her against his chest, stroking her cheek, her shoulders, her back.

"I was so scared," she whispered tear-fully.

"Shh, shh. I know. But you came through it like a pro, and everybody's safe."

"I love you."

"I know."

"I mean I really do."

"I know. I love you too, Cyn."

She wanted to tell him that he *didn't* know. She wasn't talking about the friend-ship kind of love, and he needed to under-stand that. But she found such relaxation in his arms that her eyes closed and she fell asleep without offering any argument.

When she woke up the following morning, he was nibbling at her ear. "Worth?"

"It had better be."

Keeping her eyes closed, she smiled. The sound of his voice, so low and so close and so precious to her, made her toes curl with happiness. "What time is it?"

"Does it matter?"

"I guess not."

"Turn over. I've done this side."

She rolled to her back. When she opened her eyes, his smiling face was bending down low over hers. He looked unshaven, tousled, and disreputably wonderful.

He even sounded disreputable when he said, "I love waking up beside a gorgeous, sexy broad."

"Then what are you doing here?"

Grinning, he pushed up her T-shirt and gazed at her rosy nakedness. "Aha! Just as I thought! Gorgeous and sexy."

"You're crazy."

"There's a reason for that."

"Oh? Bad genes?"

"I'm a bit teched because I've been lying here so hard for so long."

She feigned astonishment. "I thought there was a tire tool in bed with us."

Enjoying the humorous exchange, he smiled lazily and drawled, "Good morning."

"Good morning."

Her words ended on a soft moan as he cupped her breast and held it raised for his descending lips. He took the center into his mouth, drew the nipple against his teeth, and finessed it with his tongue until Cyn was gasping and clutching handfuls of his mussed hair.

His beard stubble rasped her skin as he lowered his head. She moved beneath him wantonly, shamelessly, as he kissed her navel and the sensitive area between it and the delta of soft brown hair.

But when he didn't stop there, shyness set in.

"Worth?" she whimpered with uncertainty, trying to close her thighs. He wouldn't have it. It came to a battle of wills, but her inhibitions were easily conquered by his gentle, loving persistence that acquainted her with a transporting expression of love.

After her first rippling climax, he applied his tongue again. "Worth, I can't."

"Yes you can."

She did. And he still wasn't finished. He French-kissed her softly, again and again, until the inferno in her womb built to volcanic proportions. The explosion left her shattered and quivering, bathed in perspiration and limp with exhaustion.

He turned her onto her stomach and stretched out above her. Brushing her damp hair off her neck, he planted a row of kisses across her nape as he spoke softly into her ear.

"I've always liked you, Cyn. From the moment we met, I thought you were sunny and funny and sweet. As our friendship developed and I got to know you better, I came to love you. Respectfully. As my best friend's faithful and loving wife.

"I've never seen a woman look more beautiful than you did when you held Brandon in your arms the day you brought him home from the hospital. I admired you for the courage you showed when Tim was killed. I treasured our friendship that held up even after he was no longer there. Something bonded us together. I never stopped to question what it was."

He straddled her legs and began massaging her shoulders and back. "Then we went to Mexico." His hands slid down her sides, from her underarms to her hips, coasting past the crescents her breasts formed against the bed.

"I swear, Cyn, I've never lusted for a woman so badly or felt so damned guilty about it. I saw you in a whole new light, saw you in a way I'd never seen you before."

He squeezed her waist between his hands and smoothed them over her derriere. They came to rest on the backs of her thighs.

"You were suddenly the most desirable woman I've ever known. I stopped thinking of you as my friend's widow or my good friend and began regarding you as a woman I wanted desperately to make love to. You were fun. Intelligent. Sensitive and caring. Sexy as hell. I fell in love," he concluded simply.

He turned her over and was alarmed to see tears streaking her cheeks. "Cyn?"

"I was wrong," she said in a voice made hoarse by emotion. "You *are* a poet."

He gathered her into his arms and showered her face with fervent kisses. "Oh, God, I love you."

"As your friend?"

His body coupled with hers. "As my everything."

* * *

The kitchen was a mess. Fresh out of the shower and wrapped in a robe, Cyn dismally regarded it from the doorway before tackling it. She was loading the dishwasher when she heard the latch on the back door rattle. She turned in time to see the door swing open and Ladonia rush in, followed by Charlie.

"What in the world—?" The saucer Cyn was holding in her hand dripped water onto the floor. "I thought you two were still on Maui."

"Change of plans," Charlie informed her as he set a suitcase inside the door, closing it quickly to shut out the chilly autumn air.

"Why?"

"To see what the trouble was," Ladonia said. "Cyn, what's going on?"

"What do you mean?"

"I tried calling you at work yesterday and they said you had left early."

"You were on your honeymoon. Why'd you call me?"

"Because we had decided to come back to the mainland and spend a few days in Las Vegas."

"Even though we couldn't reach you to

tell you, we flew on to Los Angeles last night," Charlie supplied.

"I called you again when we got to our hotel, and still couldn't reach you, even though it was very late here. I left several messages on the machine."

"I forgot to look," Cyn admitted sheepishly.

"Where were you last night? I tried calling Worth to ask about you, but he wasn't home either. This morning I tried this phone and it stayed busy for over two hours."

"Well, I . . . I wanted to sleep late," she stammered. Worth had lifted the phone off the hook during an intermission in their marathon of lovemaking.

"That's when I decided to call your answering service," Ladonia said. "The operator told me you'd gotten a call from a policeman last night."

Charlie chimed in again. "Ladonia about collapsed in LAX when she heard that. On the spur of the moment, we decided to hitch a plane to Dallas instead of Las Vegas."

"Oh, you shouldn't have!" Cyn exclaimed. "Everything's fine. The call from the policeman was regarding a client from the hospital."

"Where's Brandon?"

"Sleeping over at the Lattimores'."

"Thank heaven you're okay," Ladonia said, leaning against her groom, who placed a supportive arm around her. "I was worried sick. I couldn't imagine—"

Cyn followed the newlyweds' astonished, gaping stares to the doorway. Worth's hair was still wet from his shower. He'd just begun to shampoo it when she left him there. Around his middle, a towel showed up as a scanty patch of white between his bare tanned torso and bare tanned thighs.

"Morning, all," he said cheerfully. "What're you two doing back? Honeymoon over so soon?"

"Worth had to, uh, stay . . . We got in so late. I . . . I was just about to start some coffee," Cyn said feebly. "Would you like breakfast? Lunch? Did they feed you on the plane? I'm not sure what's here. I didn't get to the store—"

"Well," Ladonia said, interrupting Cyn's babbling, "I probably should give you tit for tat and repeat the sermon you gave me about having a man in the house, et cetera, but I'm too delighted that it's finally come about." She glanced up at Charlie. "I win."

"Win?" Cyn asked.

"I owe her a hundred bucks."

"I bet him that you and Worth were crazy about each other and just didn't realize it yet. I was right," Ladonia said, her eyes sparkling.

"It was getting each of them to bring a date to our wedding that did the trick," Charlie remarked.

"Mother! You manipulated us like that?"

"Well, you weren't doing too well on your own, were you?"

"Thanks, Ladonia." Worth sauntered toward Cyn and placed his arm around her waist. "I'm not apologizing for spending the night with your daughter, but I want you and Charlie to know that my intentions are honorable. We're getting married."

"We are?" Cyn asked, surprised. "Since when?"

"Did I forget to ask?" He drew her into the circle of his arms. "Cyn, will you marry me and be my best friend and only lover for life?"

In answer, she placed her arms around his neck and welcomed the heat of his mouth on hers. Their kiss was giving and greedy. Her body became pliant and receptive to the pressure his exerted.

Coming to his senses, Worth pulled back. With one hand he secured the towel he was wearing and clasped her hand with the other, leading her toward the door. To Ladonia and Charlie he said, "You'll have to excuse us. We're much better at this if we do it when the mood strikes us."

Epilogue

"Daddy, how long before Mom comes out?"

"Shouldn't be too much longer," Worth replied, ruffling Brandon's hair. It still came as a pleasant little shock to his system each time Brandon called him Daddy.

The first time had been soon after he and Cyn married. "You know, Brandon," he had said, speaking gently, "Tim McCall was really your dad."

"Yeah, I know, but he died." Brandon screwed up his face, puzzling through it, before beaming a smile up to Worth. "I'll just have two. Him when I was a baby. And you from now on."

"You can't ask for better than that," Worth had said, drawing Brandon into his arms for a hug. Cyn, who had overheard the conversation, smiled mistily at her husband over Brandon's head.

Three months into his marriage, Worth learned he was to become a father in his own right. He had waited anxiously in this same office—*not* Dr. Josh Masters'—while Cyn underwent a gynecological examination that confirmed what they had hopefully suspected.

He'd reacted with adorable foolishness, taking her out to dinner, then making stirring, tender love to her that night, whispering endearments to her and his child.

He could hardly wait for a baby to occupy the spare bedroom in their new home, which they'd purchased after selling Cyn's house and the "pleasure palace." To anybody who would listen, he touted Cyn's maternal capabilities and waxed eloquent on the offspring she was cultivating. He became a self-proclaimed expert on prenatal life and bored everyone with an encyclopedia of memorized trivia.

Ladonia told him he was the most thoroughly obsessed expectant father she'd ever run across, but he only hugged her and accused her and Charlie of being just as obsessed—which was true.

For all his braggadocio, Worth, like all conscientious new fathers, was intimidated by, even fearful of, the mystique surrounding pregnancy and birth. That's why he wasn't nearly as composed now as he pretended to be for Brandon's benefit.

He squirmed in his chair. He glanced anxiously at his wristwatch and was alarmed to see how long Cyn had been in the examination room. This was supposed to have been a routine checkup. Quick in, quick out. That's why he and Brandon had tagged along, with plans to go to the movies after her appointment.

What was taking so long? Was something wrong?

Something was wrong.

"I'm thirsty," Brandon complained.

"Hang in there. It can't take much longer."

"But Mom's been in there forever."

"She has, hasn't she?"

They had exhausted most of the books in the waiting room, but at the bottom of the stack, Worth found a Bible story they had overlooked. "You'll like this," he told the restless boy. "This is about a guy who gets swallowed by a whale."

"Jonah."

"Hey, I'm impressed."

He began to read aloud. But no sooner had the disobedient prophet got in the belly of the whale than Cyn emerged from the warren of examination rooms through a frosted-glass door.

Worth looked at her expectantly. To his supreme irritation, she avoided his inquiring eyes.

"Ready for the movies?" she asked her son.

Brandon slung aside the Bible storybook, scrambled out of his chair, and raced for the door. They followed him outside.

"Everything okay?" Worth asked worriedly.

"Everything's fine."

He held the car door for Brandon while he climbed into the backseat, but he stepped in front of Cyn, blocking her from getting in. "Something's wrong."

"No there's not," she insisted with a firm shake of her head.

"Cyn, you're a lousy liar. What's wrong?"

"Nothing's *wrong*," she said, emphasizing the word.

"Then what is it you're not telling me?"

"I was just waiting for the right moment."

"This is the right moment."

She drew a deep breath. "Well, you know how much I wanted a baby, your baby," she said gently, curving her hand around the back of his neck.

"Is that why you made me do it twice a day and three times on Sundays?"

She could maintain her withering gaze only so long before the joy bubbling inside her escaped in the form of a laugh. "You know how Mother is always warning me to be careful what I wish for?"

"Because you might get more than you bargained for."

"Hmm."

He studied her mysteriously twinkling eyes for several seconds before his own eyes sharpened with a burst of clarity and profound delight. "Twins?"

"Triplets."

About the Author

SANDRA BROWN is the author of more than fifty *New York Times* bestsellers, with over seventy million copies of her books in print. She and her family divide their time between South Carolina and Texas.